TRINITY STONE

TRINITY STONE

THE WITCH OF THE SEA

JESS GRAY

Lumen Artery Publishing

Published by Lumen Artery Publishing

Ridgway, Colorado

Illustrations Copyright © 2021 by Jess Gray

Copyright © 2021 by Jess Gray

ISBN: 978-1-7377558-0-7

www.lumenartery.com

First Printing, 2021

www.jessgray.com

In loving memory of Granny Gray, thank you for cultivating a lifetime of reading and writing, you are my angel. I'll forever love you to the moon and back.

1111

Table of Contents

1

LOACH

To the people of Elsinore, Crown Castle was the symbol of grandeur and wealth. A towering masterpiece of imposing red brick, gracefully curving terraces, sweeping gables, and ornamental portals and windows that overlooked the crashing waves of the sea, the home of my grandfather, King Eric Kronborg, was as epic as the ocean itself.

But to me, it was more like a prison.

The windows in the study were to remain closed at all times, according to my grandfather's orders. But I cracked one open anyway to take a peek at the storm brewing out on the horizon. I couldn't help it; the castle felt especially glum today. Maybe because the weather had been just like this on that fateful day almost two years ago when the sea had carried away my parents.

I tucked a strand of black hair behind my ear, gazing at the waves crashing onto the rocks far below. The impact sent the cool sting of saltwater high in the air, misting my skin. I always loved watching the storm-tossed waves breaking over the pier and crashing onto the stone gate. Yet another thing that caused people to wonder about me, to whisper thoughts that quickly grew into rumors. I went from being Ursula Violet Kronborg, the poor orphan whose mother and father had drowned, to the strange girl with an unhealthy obsession with the ocean.

It was true that what had happened to my parents didn't make me fear the sea. Quite the opposite. Sometimes I fantasized about those waves turning into arms, reaching into the castle windows, and carrying me off to find Mom and Dad.

It does sound strange, doesn't it? Ask anyone in Elsinore.

A rumble sounded in the distance as the blue-black clouds on the horizon raced across the sea towards the isle. Several bolts of lightning followed, and seconds later, the sky opened up and sheets of frigid rain poured down.

I was mesmerized. I could practically see myself down below, sprinting out of the castle and straight

2

across the beach into the waves, allowing the ocean to envelop me in a welcoming embrace.

See? I *was* pretty strange. Even I had to admit it.

I wasn't the graceful young princess and future queen the people of Elsinore wanted me to be. I tripped over my own two feet constantly. I stumbled over my words, too. My light purple eyes alone were enough to startle anyone when they first saw me up close.

My cousin Tristan always reassured me that my eyes made me special. Whenever someone teased me about them, he would tell me an old fairy tale his mother told him when we were little. It was a silly story about a mystical amethyst with extraordinary powers guarded by sea otters, of all creatures. Dear Aunt Isla loved sea otters. "So cute, but so fierce," she always said.

But when Tristan told the story, he would always point out that my eyes were the exact color of that amethyst stone. If I was being honest, I liked them, too. That was why I went by my middle name, Violet—the color of my eyes.

Maybe the people of Elsinore could have gotten used to my eyes. Maybe they could have even admired them, one day. Maybe I would grow out of my awkwardness and become graceful and worthy of their respect.

Maybe all of that could have come to pass. But

after what happened on my last birthday? No way. Now they all believed I was a witch.

Thunder boomed again, and my fingers twitched on the curtains. I so badly wanted to run out into the storm. But if I so much as stuck my toe outside the castle doors, the full entourage of guards and servants Grandfather had ordered to keep me safe would no doubt surround me.

"Ahem."

With a gasp, I whirled around. "Cora! You gave me such a fright," I cried, placing a hand to my chest.

The lanky, auburn-haired girl smiled at me from the doorway. She took a step forward, carefully balancing the tray of tea in her hands, and promptly tripped over the edge of the gold door wedge.

She caught herself just in time, barely managing not to spill the tea. I hid a grin. My maid was one of the most coordinated girls I'd ever met—possibly from saving me from all of my mishaps—she was forced to stay on point at all times. Cora was also the jolliest person in Crown Castle, from her always rosy cheeks to her boisterous laugh that could be heard from any wing.

"Sorry about that, Miss Violet," Cora said, setting down the tray and hurrying over to the window. "But if you don't start focusing on your work, the king will have my head on a chopping block!"

I rolled my eyes. Cora was my teacher, but she

knew as well as I did that Grandfather would never punish her. She and her mother, Sirena, the castle's head chef, were the only two people that could make Eric Kronborg crack a smile these days. Not even me or Tristan could get a laugh out of him. He was too busy fretting over our safety.

It has been like this for the last two years. And while it had started with my parents' disappearance, our family's misfortune hadn't ended there. A plague had swept through Elsinore not long after, leaving my aunt and uncle dead and poor Tristan confined to a wheelchair.

And it was all my fault, if you believed the rumors. After all, I was the only one still alive and in good health.

"Eric Kronborg is miserably cursed."

"It's that granddaughter of his. She's the only one in that family who isn't sick or dead!"

"She's a witch, I tell you. Those purple eyes give me the heebie-jeebies!"

"Don't forget what happened during that awful storm on her tenth birthday. Saw what she was doing with my own eyes. Unnatural, that girl."

The worst part about that last one was that my own memories of what happened during that storm are practically nonexistent. I didn't know if what people claim they saw was true because I couldn't remember! Whenever I thought about how I ran across that field, when I really tried to focus on everything that came next, I saw an explosion of red lightning over a dark and turbulent sea…then darkness.

I couldn't blame anyone for thinking the Kronborgs were cursed. Sometimes, I even believed it myself. But it struck me as horribly unfair to think that I was the only one unaffected. I'd lost my parents and my aunt and uncle. I'd suffered as much as anyone. Why couldn't they see that?

Cora shooed me away from the window, and I reluctantly headed back to the stiff armchair and table where a stack of textbooks waited. Slouching down, I watched the steam curl over the cup of chamomile tea and sighed.

"Do I have to do my compositions today?" I asked. "Maybe I could have the day off as an early birthday present?"

Cora chuckled. "Now, Miss Violet, do you really think the fact that you're almost eleven years old will get you out of doing your homework? Come now," she said, picking up my notebook and placing it on my lap. "Three pages, and no less. I'll be back to check on you in an hour—I'm off to feed Flotsam and Jetsam. And drink some of that tea!" she added as she hurried back to the door. "There's an awful draft in here."

With that, she was gone. I glared down at my notebook. I adored Cora, I really did, but she was such a stickler for the rules. Here I was, stuck in my study room all alone. Tristan was off studying in another room in the castle because, heaven forbid, we be allowed to study together. (In all fairness, Cora was probably right to keep us apart—Tristan was just as much of a rule-breaker as I was, and his wheelchair didn't stop him from exploring and occasionally getting into trouble.)

But couldn't Cora at least let me have the company of my pups while I studied? Having Flotsam curled up at my feet while Jetsam took his customary place snuggled under the crook of my arm would definitely make writing this three-page composition more enjoyable.

Heaving a sigh, I picked up the fountain pen lying next to the tea tray and opened my notebook. But I'd barely written a word when:

THUD.

I dropped the pen, sitting up in alarm. The sound had come from the beach, and it definitely wasn't thunder.

THUD. THUD. THUD.

Alarmed, I tossed my notebook aside and sprinted to the window. Yanking back the curtains, I pressed my face to the glass. It took several seconds before I realized what I was looking at.

Dozens of servants were walking from the castle to the gate, backs bent to the sheets of rain, pushing enormous carts stacked with giant gray stones, each carved into a perfectly smooth rectangle—exactly like the gate's stones. Each time a cart reached the gate, the servants pushing it would tip it over, and...

THUD.

The stones would topple onto the sand, adding to a quickly growing pile. Then the servants would wheel the empty cart back to the castle.

My heart began to beat so hard I could feel it in my throat. It looked as though they were going to add more stones to the gate. But why? Already, it was too high for any intruder to scale. We were perfectly safe in the castle.

I had seen old plans for a wall once. Tristan had found it in the library: blueprints, the paper yellowed and brittle, with sketches of the castle grounds completely encircled by a wall.

"It's from the war," he told me excitedly, smoothing the blueprints out on the table. Tristan loved anything to do with history or mythology. "The war against the Dark Ones. Grandfather had it drawn up as a sort of back-up plan, before he joined forces with Poseidon, in case the Dark Ones invaded."

"Good thing," I said, giving the blueprints a quick glance before returning to my book. "A wall like that would be a terrible eyesore."

I stared at the servants wheeling more stones out, along with sacks of cement. The war against the Dark

Ones had ended before I was born. They were gone, banished forever. There was no need to build a wall like that. There was no enemy to keep out.

Then it hit me. Grandfather wasn't worried about what was outside of the castle. He was worried about what was inside.

Me.

My fingers gripped the curtains until my knuckles turned white. Grandfather had been more anxious than usual lately. Just yesterday at breakfast when Tristan had mentioned my upcoming birthday party, Grandfather had dropped the butter dish on poor Jetsam's head.

Grandfather hadn't looked at me quite the same since what happened on my tenth birthday. He never called me a witch, at least, not outright. But something had changed in our relationship.

And now, as my eleventh birthday approached, he was building a wall.

Whatever the servants were doing to the gate had something to do with me, I was sure of it. And I wasn't going to sit around and wait to see what it was.

Leaving the curtains wide open, I turned and raced out of the room.

2

CEMENT WALLS

My grandfather was a kind man and a good king. The war against the Dark Ones had changed him, according to everyone—even my parents. Mom described it as an extra shadow that clung to him.

"He never was quite the same after that," she would say wistfully. "There is a darkness, a cloud that hangs over him that he can't quite seem to shake off."

I could tell it made her sad, which made me feel sad, too.

Of course, I'd only ever known that version of Grandfather. I loved him—really, I did. But I didn't just lose my parents two years ago. I lost him, too.

Because now I knew exactly how my mother had felt. Her death, and my father's death, had broken the king even more. He wasn't quite the same grandfather I had known growing up.

I tried to remind myself of this as I sprinted down the hall to his chambers. But with every locked door I passed, with every portrait and painting draped in dusty old cloth to hide any glimpse of my parents' faces or ships or water or *any* reminder of that day I saw, my anger only grew.

I understood that Grandfather was in a state of inconsolable grief since the loss of his son and daughter-in-law. But what about *my* grief? I lost my parents. Then I lost my aunt and uncle. Then I had lost my freedom.

The entire west wing of Crown Castle was forbidden. Grandfather had locked the entrance to the hall not even a week after Mom and Dad vanished, and without a word of explanation. I was devastated, because the west wing had the best views of the ocean, but I didn't argue. More than once, Tristan and I had whispered plans about sneaking in and taking a look around, but we never followed through. We figured that surely Grandfather would come around after a few months.

Instead, his paranoia only seemed to grow with each passing day. And I didn't think I could stand his overprotectiveness much longer.

I raced past the two guards flanking the doors to the council chambers and burst inside. Grandfather was seated at the head of the long table, as always. He looked up wearily when I entered, his advisors' heads swiveling in my direction. I heard a few murmurs of disapproval at my decorum, but I ignored them.

"What are your men doing to the gate?" I demanded, hands on my hips.

To Grandfather's right, Emil Jensen stiffened, his waxed mustache twitching with indignation. "Young lady, you'd do well to remember that you're addressing your king."

"And you'd do well to remember you're addressing your future queen," I retorted, watching with savage pleasure as Emil's pale face turned beetroot red. Grandfather trusted his senior advisor above all others, but I never did like him much. My gut instinct churns, lurches and blazes like wild fire when I see him. He is a peasant that made his way to the top, I see him for who he really is, a rat. And his breath smelled like tuna that had been left out of the ice box for too long. The feeling was obviously mutual. His lip curled every time he looked at me, like I was a grubby worm that had managed to crawl inside from the gardens.

"Violet," Grandfather said quietly. There wasn't a trace of anger in his voice—there never was, not these days—but a hush fell instantly over the room. I stopped in my tracks, squeezing my hands into fists, and glowered at him. Sighing, Grandfather looked around the table. "Council adjourned, for now. We'll resume our meeting after lunch."

The moment the doors clicked closed behind them, the words burst out of me.

"Are you trying to make the gate stronger?" I demanded. "Is it because you think I'll sneak out? Already, I can't go to the beach without a dozen guards watching my every move."

Grandfather gazed at me silently, twisting the ruby ring on his right hand—a nervous tic he'd developed over the last year or so. His silvery hair and beard were more salt than pepper. Before my parents vanished, his hair was dark brown with just a few streaks of gray, and his face was youthful, his laugh loud and booming. Now, it seemed like each week that passed left him with another wrinkle or worry line.

I lowered my voice. "Do you not trust me, Grandfather?"

Grandfather closed his eyes briefly and sighed. "Violet, my dear, it isn't you I don't trust."

I frowned. What did that mean? Elsinore didn't have any enemies; we hadn't for decades, not since the war against the Dark Ones. We lived in peaceful times. Before I could ask him to explain, he continued.

"A few nights ago, I couldn't sleep," Grandfather said. "So, I took a stroll on the grounds. It was a clear night, and I happened to glance up at your window."

Every muscle in my body froze. I knew exactly what he had seen because I did the same thing every night. It was the only privacy I had, the only time when I was truly alone and could do as I pleased.

"There you were, my beautiful granddaughter, future queen of this land, sitting on a ledge a dozen stories off the ground, legs dangling, staring at the sea as if under some wicked spell."

His voice hardened slightly on the last few words. I lifted my chin and met his gaze.

"Was I doing something wrong?"

Grandfather sat forward, fixing me with his pale blue eyes. "You could have fallen, for one thing. But I find it even more concerning that your obsession with the ocean continues. Especially after what happened last year."

A heavy silence settled over the room. Grandfather looked at me as if I was a foe, guilty of a crime. I ignored the flush creeping up my neck and met Grandfather's eyes.

"It's not an obsession," I argued half-heartedly. In truth, though, he was right. I hadn't been allowed to set foot in the sea in a year, but no one could stop me from looking at it. I found it hypnotic: a whole world just beyond, a magical place filled with wonders and endless possibilities spread out beneath the crashing waves.

Grandfather's silvery brows knitted together as he watched me. "It's not your fault, my dear," he murmured, almost more to himself than to me. "The temptation proves to be too much for you to resist."

Emil walked back into the room uninvited and stood by grandfather's chair like a statue.

My mouth opened and closed. "What are you talking about?" I finally managed to ask. "What temptation?"

But the king's eyes had already slid out of focus, his fingers back to compulsively twisting the ruby ring. A cold, prickly feeling shivered up my spine and down my arms, causing the hairs on the back of my neck to stand up. After nearly a minute of silence, I couldn't bear it any longer.

"Grandfather?"

He blinked, his gaze falling onto me. Then he placed both hands flat on the table and stood, his arms quaking slightly with the effort.

"I have ordered my men to build a wall," Grandfather said, his tone flat and emotionless. "They will extend the gate's height to fifty feet, blocking all views of the sea from the castle and completely enclosing the grounds. The only access to the beach will be the gate's entrance, which will have two guards stationed around the clock."

"*What?!*"

The word came out too high, too shrill, ringing off the stone walls. Panic spread through me, a red-hot fire that felt as though my skeleton was trying to claw its way out of my skin.

"Violet, the ocean is a dangerous place," Grandfather said. "But nothing, not even the death of your own parents, has been enough to convince you of that fact."

"But I—"

"Out of sight, out of mind," he went on, as if I hadn't said a word. "You will not look at the ocean. You will not think of the ocean. You will not dream of the ocean. You will focus on your studies and on becoming the queen Elsinore expects you to be— the queen they will one day *need* you to be. Do you understand me?"

I dug my fingernails into my palms. "Yes," I managed to choke out.

"Good." Grandfather sank back down into his chair. "Now, return to your lessons. I have a meeting to finish."

Turning, I stalked towards the doors, my vision blurry with tears. Once in the hall, I broke into a run.

But I didn't go back to my study. There was no way I could write a composition now. I needed to talk to the only person in this entire castle—on this entire *isle*—who truly understood me. And there was only one place he could possibly be.

I burst into the royal library, causing the doors to slam against the walls and sending a few books toppling from their shelves. Tristan looked up from his usual table, green eyes wide with alarm. He shoved the black book he'd been reading beneath a larger blue leather-bound book before realizing it was me.

"Violet? What's wrong?"

I told him everything, hot tears streaming down my face as I paced back and forth. Slowly, Tristan clasped his hands on the cover of the blue book. The gold-printed letters read *ADVANCED ASTRONOMY: MAPPING AND CHARTING THE STARS.*

When I finished, Tristan shook his head slowly.

"I'm worried about Grandfather," he said, drumming his fingers on the astronomy book. "Being protective of us is one thing, but to completely surround the castle with a wall like that...he's paranoid. It's gone too far."

"It's not just protectiveness." I slumped down in the chair across from him, wiping my wet cheeks with the back of my hand. "And it's not *us*. It's *me*. He doesn't trust me, Tristan. It's like he thinks I'm... you know."

A witch.

Tristan reached across the table and grabbed my hands. "He doesn't think that, Violet. He loves you!

He's just afraid of losing you."

I tried to smile as I squeezed his hands back. But I couldn't forget the distant look in Grandfather's eyes, the odd words he'd spoken. *It's not your fault. The temptation proves too much for you to resist.*

"I guess it doesn't matter why he's doing it," I said glumly, letting go of Tristan's grip and leaning back in my chair. "When that wall is finished, I won't be able to see the ocean ever again." My voice broke, and I closed my eyes.

Tristan was silent for a long moment. "That's not necessarily true," he said finally.

I opened my eyes. My cousin's normally pale face was flushed with excitement, and his lips twitched up in a mischievous smile I knew all too well. "What are you up to?" I asked, sitting up straight.

Tristan glanced around the empty library. "Well... I've been reading this."

He slid the black book out from beneath the blue one. There was no title on the cover, just a small gold triangle in the center that shimmered enticingly. I frowned, glancing at the spine, but there was no title there, either.

"Why'd you hide it when I came in?"

"I thought you were Cora. Or worse, Sirena."

I snorted. "Since when would you get in trouble for *reading*?" My cousin constantly had his nose buried in a book. History, mythology, geography...all stuff that would put me to sleep, but Tristan gobbled it all up.

Leaning forward, Tristan grinned at me. "Pretty sure I'd get in plenty of trouble reading a book of spells."

That got my attention. I gaped at him, then studied the book again. "Spells? As in…*magic*?"

He nodded excitedly. "At least, I'm pretty sure. It's kind of hard to read."

"You found it in the library?"

Tristan laughed. "Are you kidding? No way!"

"So, where'd you get it, then?"

Now his eyes were sparkling mischievously. "Well, I was going to save this for a birthday surprise, but I—"

"Miss Violet!"

The two of us swiveled around to face the entrance, Tristan shoving the black book with the gold triangle back underneath the astronomy tome. Cora stood there, hands on her hips and a mock stern expression on her rosy face. Her eyes softened as soon as she saw my tear-stained cheeks.

"Oh, dear," she said, bustling over and crouching down next to my chair. Carefully, she dabbed at my face with the edge of her apron. "There, there, now," she said softly. "It'll all be okay, Miss Violet."

I swallowed hard, suddenly too tired to argue. Nothing would be okay. Not while I had a grandfather determined to keep me locked away from the world.

"It's this gloomy weather, no doubt," Cora said, pulling me to my feet. "Forget the tea—how about I fix you up a nice mug of hot cocoa while you finish that composition? I'll bring you a cup, too, Tristan!" she added over her shoulder as she gently shooed me from the library.

"Sure, thanks!" Tristan paused, then added, "It's okay, Violet. I'll give you your present later."

I glanced back and caught a glimpse of him giving me a wink and a grin before the library door swung closed.

He'd gotten me a birthday surprise. As much as I appreciated that, even the thought of birthday presents couldn't cheer me up right now. Cora kept up a steady stream of chatter the whole way back to my study, but I barely heard a word. All I could think about was a future of nothing but stone and cement.

That night, no less than a minute after Cora had drawn my bath and left my chambers, there was a soft, rhythmic knock on my door.

Tap. Tap-tap-tap. Tap.

"Tristan," I whispered, recognizing our secret knock right away. I hurried across my bedroom and pulled the door open.

Tristan didn't say a word until he'd wheeled inside, and the door was firmly closed once more. "Ready for your present?"

I pulled my robe tighter around me. "Now?"

"Sure! Why not?"

"It's after dark!" I said, a feeble attempt at a protest. But despite my foul mood, a little spark of excitement flared up in the pit of my belly.

Tristan grinned. "Exactly. Let's just say Grandfather wouldn't approve of this gift."

Now I was grinning, too, all my fear and despair about the wall momentarily forgotten. Whatever Tristan was going to show me, it was clearly no ordinary birthday present.

3

PASSAGES

I hurried into my closet to change into something a little more appropriate for sneaking around the castle than my nightgown and slippers. Then Tristan and I left my chambers as silently as possible and made our way down the hall.

We didn't speak at all; the night guards tended to stick to the entrances on the first floor, but we'd had close run-ins with servants taking care of a few last chores before retiring for the evening.

In all honesty, I liked Crown Castle best at night. I was never really frightened of the dark, and I knew every nook and cranny of the castle so that each shadow or creak was as familiar as my own hand. The eastern wing had three floors, and my bed chamber was on the third, along with Grandfather's, Tristan's, and what used to be my parents' chambers. There were several guest rooms as well, though I couldn't remember the last time anyone had slept in them. The kitchen and dining hall could be found on the second floor, along with the various meeting rooms for the king and his council. The first floor was taken up largely by the ballroom that would be the site of my party tomorrow—a thought that made my stomach sour, so I pushed it aside—along with the library and a few sitting rooms no one used these days.

A stairway in the southeast corner connected the third floor to the second and first floor. When Grandfather realized Tristan would be wheelchair-bound permanently, he installed a ramp to run alongside the stairs. More than once, I'd slid all the way down on the railing alongside Tristan while Cora chided me from the foyer, even though I could tell she was trying not to laugh.

The west wing of the castle was far more interesting, in my opinion. Mostly because unlike the east wing, it was off-limits to the public. The king might throw lavish parties or invite important guests over for dinner, but all of that took place in the east wing. The west wing was for the royal family only. Even the servants had very limited access.

There were bathhouses, several of them, each with

marble floors and great big bathtubs that faced giant windows overlooking the sea. The barbican at the top was open-air and offered an even more breathtaking view, not just of the sea but of Elsinore itself, the rows of copper-roofed homes and all the shops and cobblestone roads. Tristan and I had spent so much time up there when we were little, playing hide-and-seek in the little garden my mother tended, chasing each other around the gazebo.

At the end of the hall, I expected Tristan to turn right and head to his chambers. I figured he must have my present hidden there. Instead, he turned left, toward the main corridor—toward the stairs.

I hurried to catch up. "Where are we going?" I mouthed, but he just grinned and shook his head. When we reached the staircase, Tristan wheeled carefully down the ramp, while I followed down the steps. As we passed the second floor, I shot Tristan a questioning look, and he responded with a mysterious smile.

On the first floor, we paused and listened hard for any sound, any sign a servant—or worse, Sirena—might be nearby. But Crown Castle was as silent as a tomb.

Tristan crooked his finger in a "follow me" motion, then wheeled past the ballroom. I trailed behind, trying not to think about tomorrow, when practically all of Elsinore would gather inside, forced to celebrate the birthday of a girl they believed to be wicked. Cursed.

I tried to focus on Tristan's surprise instead. My curiosity grew with every step. Where in the world were we going? We'd just passed the library, the only other rooms at the end of this hall were various sitting rooms filled with antique furniture and old portraits. After that, the hall was a dead-end, the locked entrance to…

I stopped in my tracks. "Tristan," I whispered, stunned. "Are we going to the west—"

A voice cut me off, low and familiar, the words muffled. Tristan and I exchanged an alarmed look and quickly stepped into the shadow of a marble statue of a knight riding a horse. I strained to hear the sounds of approaching footsteps over the rapid *boom-boom-boom* of my heart. Then Tristan touched my arm.

"Look," he mouthed, pointing to the double doors directly opposite the statue. I peered around the knight's back and saw it—the dim glow of candlelight barely visible beneath the doors.

Exhaling, I moved around the statue and crept carefully toward the doors, Tristan at my side. I pressed my ears to the thick oak, trying to identify the voice, but it was no use.

Tristan tugged at my sleeve. When I looked at him, he nodded down the hall. I glanced over, my gaze falling on the entrance to the library, and I immediately understood.

Without a word, we crept back up the corridor until we reached the library. I tugged on the handle, relieved when the door swung open. I couldn't imagine why it would be locked at night, but with Grandfather's increasing paranoia, it wouldn't have surprised me.

The moment we were inside, the door safely shut behind us, Tristan let out a sigh of relief.

"That sounded like Emil," he said as we made our way expertly through the stacks.

Startled, I realized he was right. "But who would he be talking to?" I wondered. "Surely not Grandfather. They'd be in the council room."

"Maybe Emil and Sirena are just having some tea and a chat," Tristan joked, and I snorted with laughter. Sirena never did try to hide her dislike of Emil, and the feeling was clearly mutual.

When we reached the wall that separated the library from the sitting room, I moved straight to the shelf in the center.

"Top shelf," Tristan said, as if I needed reminding. I stood on my tiptoes and scanned the books along the top shelf until I spotted it: a slate gray leather book with the words *A HISTORY OF PASSAGES* stamped in silver down the binding. Feeling a little echo of the thrill I'd felt when Tristan and I had first made this discovery, I reached out and grabbed the book and pulled.

Shhhhh-THUNK. Shhhhh-THUNK. Shhhhh-THUNK.

Stepping back, I listened to the muffled sounds of great big gears turning behind the shelf. It wasn't audible in the sitting room—Tristan and I had tested that out years ago just to be sure. In all honesty, we never overheard anything particularly juicy in all our little spy missions; just the maids gossiping, mostly, although once we were treated to Cora belting out a sea shanty while she dusted the furniture. The lyrics, along with her charmingly off-key singing, had Tristan and I curled up on the ground clutching our stomachs, tears of silent laughter streaming down our faces.

CLACK.

The shelf swung open a few inches. Tristan grabbed it and pulled it open wide enough for his wheelchair to fit through. I followed him into the dark passage, adrenaline coursing through me.

I supposed calling it a passage was kind of an exaggeration. It was more of a hiding spot inside the wall, longer and wider than a bathtub, but not by much. There was a wooden door on the other side, and Tristan pulled it open slowly and with great care. On the other side was canvas—the backside of a life-size portrait of the king. That canvas was the only thing separating Tristan and I from the sitting room. Everything was audible—and if we made so much as a peep, Emil would hear us, too. I didn't want to think about what he would do if he caught us spying.

"He's unwell," a raspy voice was saying. I vaguely recognized it as belonging to another member of the king's council, a tall, reedy-looking man with a pointy goatee. "Has been for some time. We must do what is best for Elsinore."

"Precisely, Rodden," came Emil's response, his tone even more pompous than usual. "And as much as it pains me to say this, the king has brought this misery on himself."

"How so?" This voice was softer, almost nervous. I recognized it, too, and conjured an image of yet another council member, this one with freckles and a shock of red hair. "I agree the king seems to suffer more by the day, but he has always put Elsinore first."

"I thought so, too," Emil said gravely. "But alas, I've recently learned that not to be the case. Ever since the war against the Dark Ones, the pact with Poseidon, the king has been keeping a grave secret from all of us. One that puts Elsinore at risk more and more every day."

A shiver ran up my spine. This wasn't fun anymore, sneaking around and spying. And it wasn't just the words he's saying—something in Emil's voice chilled me right to the bone.

"Let me guess," said Rodden. "This secret involves our future... *queen*."

He spat the last word out with such distaste, I found myself recoiling in shock. I was so taken aback by his vehemence, I couldn't even muster so much as a whiff of outrage. Next to me, Tristan's face had gone pale as the moon, his eyes wide and unblinking behind his glasses.

"It does," Emil agreed softly. "The girl is a ticking time bomb. Already, everyone in Elsinore suspects the truth about her. All this past year, I thought the king simply couldn't admit it, was too blinded by love for his granddaughter. But the real truth is far, far worse."

For an endless moment, the world seemed to go mute. I didn't move, didn't breathe. Just waited for Emil's next words.

Then, three things happened in quick succession.

From inside the library, someone called out, "Yoo-hoo! Anyone in here?"

Tristan gasped and rolled back—right over my foot.

And cry of pain escaped my lips before I could hold it back.

I clapped my hands over my mouth, but it was too late. The men on the other side of the canvas had gone dangerously quiet. Tristan met my gaze, and I saw my own panic reflected in his eyes.

We had to get out of here, *now.*

I hurried out of the passage, Tristan right behind me. Together, we pushed the secret shelf door closed as quietly as possible. Then we started to make our way to the doors as quickly as possible—until the sound of footsteps caused us to freeze.

"Who's in here?" It was Rodden towering in the doorway. Tristan and I huddled out of sight behind the shelf, not daring to breathe.

"Oh!" A high, fluttery laugh came from the other side of the library. A maid moved into the main aisle, hand to her chest, a feather duster in her hand. "Goodness, you startled me, sir! I was passing by and saw the library was open, so I thought I'd make sure no one was in here before I locked up."

I crouched a little to get a better look at Rodden's face between the stacks. "This place empty?"

The maid looked nervous now, probably because she was facing a clearly angry member of the king's council. "I checked this side, sir," she said, nodding back in the direction she came. "Was just about to check that side."

She pointed at the far-right wall—directly at our secret passage.

Without a word, Rodden stormed off toward the wall. For a long, excruciating moment, the maid simply stood in the same spot, blocking the main aisle—me and Tristan's only path to escape.

Then she scurried after him. The moment she disappeared down the aisle, Tristan and I bolted.

As soon as we were out the doors, I grabbed the handles of Tristan's wheelchair and pushed, running as fast as I could, never mind about the noise. I didn't dare look back for fear I'd see Emil hot on my heels—but I suspected he'd stayed in the sitting room, sending the reedy-looking man to scope out the noise. And thankfully, no one called out after us.

I didn't slow down my pace as I pushed Tristan up the ramp to the second floor, then the third. By the time I reached his chambers, I had a stitch in my side.

"What was that?" I gasped, hardly able to breathe. "Emil…what was he talking about?"

Tristan looked unnerved. "I don't know, but all that stuff about Grandfather being unwell, it sounded like…" He paused, gulping. "Violet, it sounded like treason."

A fresh wave of fear rippled through me, cold and sharp. We stared at one another for a long moment, neither of us sure what to say next. Then Tristan seemed to snap to attention.

"They heard us," he said. "Even if they don't find the secret passage, they know someone overheard them. They'll search the castle to see who isn't where they should be."

I knew what he meant. I needed to get back to my chambers as fast as possible. But I didn't want to be

31

alone, not after what we'd just heard.

"Tristan—"

"Violet, you have to hurry," Tristan said urgently. "If they catch us together—if they even catch us awake…"

He was right. I knew he was right. With a last, desperate glance at my cousin, I fled his room.

I flew down the corridor toward my chambers. Was that the sound of footsteps on the stairs, or just my pulse pounding in my ears? I couldn't bring myself to look over my shoulder as I reached my room, closed the doors, and sprinted to my closet. Trembling from head to foot, I changed back into my nightgown as fast as I could, then dove beneath the covers.

Half a minute later, my door creaked open.

I lay there, hot and sweaty, struggling to keep my breathing slow and even. I could feel the stare, even if I had no idea who it was checking up on me— the maid, I hoped, and not Emil. After what felt like ages, the door clicked closed softly.

I lowered the covers and drew in a deep breath. I was alone now, safe in my bed.

Only I had never felt less safe in my entire life.

4

Red Lightening

That night, my dreams were filled with water.
I glided through the waves, allowing the current to guide my way. Beneath the surface, the sea was a glittering turquoise wonderland so dazzling it caused my heart to ache. But every few seconds, when I'd break the surface to take another breath, I'd spot a dark cloud on the horizon, and Emil's words would echo like distant thunder.

The girl is a ticking time bomb.

The dark cloud was nothing but a speck at first, but it grew a little bit bigger each time I came up for air.

Already, everyone in Elsinore suspects the truth

about her.

I dove beneath the waves, then emerged once again.

But the real truth is far, far worse.

And then, at last, I saw it wasn't a cloud at all.

A massive creature was rising up from the ocean. Already, its head was in the clouds, so all I could see was its wide black body...and then one by one, thick tentacles rose around it like giant, charmed snakes, twisting and undulating and reaching for the sky before slamming back down onto the sea with an almighty *SPLASH!*

With a gasp, I sat up straight in bed. Blood pounded in my ears as I struggled to catch my breath. My skin tingled with lingering excitement over the vision of the mighty creature. To any other child, this would probably qualify as a nightmare. But in my dream, I hadn't been frightened of the creature.

I was in awe at its power.

Throwing the blankets off, I swung my legs over the side of my bed and stretched. Everything that had happened last night—sneaking out with Tristan, the secret passage, the awful things Emil had said—it all felt like a dream, too.

It sounded like treason. Remembering Tristan's words, I shivered and pulled my robe on and stuck my feet in my purple slippers. It wasn't until I'd entered my bathing chambers that I remembered I was eleven years old today.

Already, the tub was filled with warm water. I imagined Cora quietly entering my room before I woke to fill the tub as she did every morning, and I wondered what I looked like lying in my bed, dreaming of the ocean.

Of that majestic creature.

After a long soak in the tub, I toweled off and headed to my closet. Last week, Cora and Sirena had surprised me with a gown for my birthday party. It was the most beautiful dress I'd ever seen: sleeveless with a full skirt, the iridescent fabric was a deep violet at the top, but lightened to ocean blue, then aquamarine, then finally emerald green near the ankles.

I'd been thrilled when I tried it on. But now, the shimmery, silky fabric just reminded me of the sea… and the wall that would soon stop me from ever laying eyes on it again.

My heart sank like a stone when I pictured the wall. How much progress had Grandfather's men made yesterday? How much time did I have left until my world turned monotone gray forever?

Another thought struck me. Did the wall have something to do with the secret Emil claimed Grandfather was keeping? I struggled to remember what else he'd said…something about the war against the Dark Ones, the pact with Poseidon…

I pondered this as I brushed my long, black hair in front of the mirror, so deep in thought that it was nearly a full minute before I noticed something was wrong.

Slowly, I lowered my hairbrush. In the mirror, my reflection blinked in confusion. A streak of silver ran through my hair, starting just above my right eye. Fingers trembling, I touched it as cautiously as though it were a dormant snake waiting to strike, rather than a lock of my own hair. The silver caught the sunlight streaming in through the window, gleaming so bright it was almost as white as Grandfather's beard.

My pulse began to race. I took several shaky steps back from the mirror and took in my reflection again. An eleven-year-old girl with silver-streaked black hair and violet eyes. If any of the townspeople didn't think I was a witch before now, surely this would convince them.

It had all but convinced *me*.

No. There was no way I was going to go to this birthday party—a mandatory "celebration" that the king was forcing the reluctant citizens of Elsinore to attend—looking like an actual, honest-to-goodness witch.

The real truth is far, far worse.

Turning, I raced back into my bed chambers and looked around wildly. Surely there had to be some way to hide the silver…ink, perhaps? That might work, but no way did I have enough in the little pot on my desk to cover the entire lock of hair.

My gaze landed on the fireplace, where last night's fire had long burned out. I hurried over and fell to my knees, tentatively touching the soot beneath the wood. It felt cool to the touch, so I slathered it all over my hands and began to work my still-shaking fingers through my hair. When I was done, I returned to the mirror and exhaled with relief. The black soot covered the silver perfectly.

I spent several minutes rinsing my hands in the basin, watching the gray water drain away. Now that my shock had faded, fear was starting to settle in. I could hide the silver streak for now, but could I hide it forever?

And why had it appeared overnight, right as I turned eleven?

Already, everyone in Elsinore suspects the truth about her.

I knew exactly what Emil had been referring to. Last year, on my tenth birthday, there had been a storm.

Storms were nothing unusual in a coastal town, but this one had been particularly wild. I woke up that morning to a crashing and booming so loud, it rang in my ears for days afterwards. It was past sunrise, but dark as night outside as I got out of bed and dashed to the window.

To my astonishment, a bolt of lightning red as blood flashed across the metal gray sky. Then another, and another.

Sprites, I'd remembered at the time. Tristan had told me about them once after reading about them in one of his mythology books. *It's said that when red lightning strikes, a great mystical creature is awakening, the heads of snakes begin to form, and a great war begins between land and sea.*

You are seriously the most bizarre human, I'd told him with a giggle. *Full of nonsense!*

How is that nonsense? Tristan had replied. *It's useful information!*

But seeing the sprites for myself, well, suddenly Tristan's mythological tale didn't seem so silly. As streaks of red flashed across the dark sky and sheets of rain poured into the tumultuous ocean, it felt more like a harbinger of doom.

I hadn't wanted a party that day. It was, after all, my first birthday without my parents, and I wasn't excited about turning ten. But Cora had bustled into my room, whisked me away from the window and the magnificent sight of the storm, and helped me get dressed.

I had pleaded with Grandfather to cancel the party due to the storm. Surely the people of Elsinore shouldn't be expected to come all the way up to the castle in this weather? But he wouldn't hear of it.

The sight of all the celebratory decorations had brought tears to my eyes. My mother had always loved that part—the décor, the food, the preparation. She said that for her, it was more fun than the party itself.

My grief for her and my father suddenly felt as sharp and new as it had the day they'd died, and I couldn't bear being in the castle another second.

I had snuck off when no one was looking, sprinting across the castle grounds in the pouring rain. I could see huddles of townspeople making their way up the path to the castle, so I stuck to the trees and stayed out of sight…until I heard a cry for help.

I remember freezing, the sound cutting straight through me in an almost supernatural way. I whirled around, trying to figure out which direction it had come from, but the chaos of the storm made it impossible.

Then I heard it again, and along with it came a flash, an image of something small, hurt, vulnerable. My leg suddenly felt pinched with pain, and my cry was lost to the storm. But even in the moment, I recognized that it wasn't *my* pain I was feeling.

It was the pain of an animal. And somehow, I could sense it.

Some instinct took hold, and I ran. Slipping, sliding down a grassy hill, out in the wide open now, barely aware of the townspeople pointing and gawking. A creature was in pain, terrible pain, and I could feel it as acutely as if it were my own. I heard a strangled cry, and I wasn't sure if it came from the poor animal, or from my own throat. My leg felt as though it was being pinched by a thousand tiny crabs, but I ran faster and faster through the pelting rain.

Distant shouts rang out around me as a crowd gathered along the path. Squinting up ahead, I saw a horse galloping toward me. She was panicked, I could tell, but I somehow knew she wasn't the creature in pain. The horse slowed as it reached me.

"Where is she?" I whispered, touching her soft face and gazing into her wide eyes.

The horse tossed her head and gave a little snuffle. I saw the fear and worry in her eyes, and even though I didn't hear anything, I somehow knew exactly what to do next.

I raced downhill towards the fence, the horse trotting at my side. Several townspeople followed, hurrying back downhill, pointing at me. I thought I could hear cries of, "*Isn't that the princess?*" and "*What in the name of Poseidon is she doing out in this storm?*"

But I ignored them all. My eyes had locked onto a heap of trash against the fence: fishing nets from the wharf, sticks and debris, all blown violently by the terrible wind of the storm.

Amidst the tangle, twitching and whinnying in

pain, was a spindly little foal.

"You're okay," I whispered, falling to my knees and untangling the nets. I winced at the deep cuts on her legs as I pulled her free. "It's all okay now."

The foal leaped up, kicking and bucking, and I laughed to see her so happy to be free. She had a fiery red mane and tail, which I'd never seen before.

"Like sprites," I said, running my hand over her mane. "That would make a good name for you, wouldn't it? Sprites?"

As if in response, the foal let out a delighted whinny.

But her mother was still agitated, and on the other side of the fence, the townspeople were crying out in horror. Beneath the *crack-boom* of the thunder, I heard another sound. A grating sound, like a giant metal monster gnashing its teeth.

As if in slow motion, I turned to look at the windmill on top of the hill. The metal blades were spinning out of control, caught up in the wind, scraping up against the structure—and then, like something out of a nightmare, the blades came loose and hurtled down the hill.

The townspeople screamed and ran, slipping and sliding in the mud. The horse nudged her foal, but the baby was having a hard time getting her footing. I stood there, watching in horror as the giant metal blades sliced through the air, aiming right at me and

Sprites—

And that's the last thing I remembered.

I couldn't explain it, not even to myself. All I know is that everything went black, and when I came to, the windmill blades were nowhere to be seen. The horse and her foal were racing back to the barn.

And I was flat on my back, looking up into the faces of the horrified townspeople.

"*Witch*," one had said grimly, and then I'd fainted.

Now, I lifted my head and gazed at my reflection. The soot masked the silver streak, but for how long? Was I going to have to smear soot in my hair every day to hide this?

Grandfather had been terrified when he'd learned about the windmill incident. My birthday celebrations had been called off and everyone sent home while I recovered. When I did, he told me the blades had barely missed me. That they'd blown off somewhere. That I must have fainted from fear, that I was lucky to be alive.

But even in my drowsy state, I knew that didn't make sense. Because if what Grandfather was saying was true, the townspeople would have looked at me with pity, not fear. They wouldn't have whispered *witch*.

And most importantly, when I'd stared at those blades hurtling through the rain towards me and the foal, I hadn't felt afraid. I probably should have, but

42

I hadn't. Instead, I'd felt a new feeling, one unlike anything I'd ever experienced. A fierce protectiveness that bordered on fury. Those blades would not harm Sprites or myself.

Then…darkness. What had happened? What had I done?

"Violet?"

Startled, I looked up as Cora entered the bathroom. Her face broke into a smile when she saw my dress.

"Oh, you look absolutely lovely," she gushed, hurrying over and giving me a hug. "Like a proper princess. Happy birthday, sweetheart."

"Thanks," I said, doing my best to smile. I should be happy, after all. It was my birthday. I was about to have a lavish party with plenty of presents and lots of delicious treats. Sunshine beamed through the windows, and I could see that the sky outside was clear blue and cloudless. Nothing like last year's storm.

But as I followed Cora from my chambers, I couldn't shake the feeling of dread slithering around my insides like a cold snake.

5

ELEVEN

"**D**id you try these custard cakes?" Tristan asked, holding his plate up. "They're amazing. Not that Sirena's ever baked anything that wasn't amazing."

I gave my cousin a half-hearted smile. We were parked next to the fireplace, him in his wheelchair, me in a stiff, tall-backed chair that still managed to be rock hard despite the velvet seat cushion. My shoulders were tense, and my neck ached from trying to maintain the perfect princess posture for the last hour.

Not that it mattered. Hundreds of people, dressed in their finest clothes, milled around the Great Hall, enjoying the buffet spread of delectable sweets Sirena had prepared. They gathered in smaller groups to chat as they ate, most of them eyeing Grandfather as he moved around the room, a few jostling one another to get closer in the hopes of exchanging a few words with the king.

Not a single one had wished me a happy birthday. Not that I cared. Actually, I would have been happy to simply be ignored, to only chat with Tristan and Cora until this awful party was over. It took all of my willpower not to touch the silver lock of hair, ensure the soot still darkened it. I knew my fingers would only wipe the soot away, but even so, the compulsion to check was all but impossible to ignore.

But I couldn't help noticing the glances, the whispers, the fearful looks. Each one was a tiny dagger thrown my way, the wound deepening with every blow.

Witch. Witch. Witch.

"Violet," Tristan said. "Violet?"

"Hmm?" I glanced over and saw the look of concern in his eyes. "Oh, I'm sorry, Tristan. I…I didn't sleep well last night."

"Me, either." Tristan glanced around. "*He's* not here."

I nodded grimly. All afternoon, I'd waited for Emil to walk into the ballroom. But he was nowhere to be seen. "I'm sure Grandfather ordered the council to be here," I whispered back. "It's odd he's not here."

"Can't say I'm not relieved, though." Tristan adjusted his glasses. "I'm still nervous he might have found out it was us spying."

"He couldn't have," I said firmly, although I couldn't be sure of that. "There's no way he could know it was us."

"Do you think he knows about the secret passage?"

I frowned, picturing the shelf. Tristan had discovered it by accident years ago by pulling out the book that happened to unlock the door. "I doubt Emil or any of the other council members have ever wanted to read *A History of Passages*," I said teasingly. "Only you are that bookish."

Tristan stuck his tongue out, and I giggled. "Hey, I never did give you that present," he said, lowering his voice.

I blinked in surprise. Between spying on Emil and the heart-stopping sprint back to the third floor, I'd completely forgotten the whole reason Tristan and I had been sneaking around to begin with.

"You mean your present wasn't spying on Emil?" I joked, and he snickered.

"Nope. It has nothing to do with hiding in a secret passage from that weasel." He paused, lips curving up in a mysterious smile. "Well, it has nothing to do with that weasel, anyway."

"Quit being so cryptic!" I said, although I was

amused. Then I pictured the black book with the gold triangle. "Is it something I can read?"

Tristan shook his head, eyes dancing. "Nope. It's not even something you can unwrap. And it's definitely not something Grandfather can know about."

Suddenly, I remembered where we'd been heading before getting distracted by the secret council meeting in the sitting room. "Is it in the west wing?" I whispered eagerly, leaning closer—and that's when I saw Emil in the entrance, staring at the two of us from across the ballroom. I gasped and pointed, knocking the plate of untouched cinnamon pumpkin tarts off the arm of my chair. "Oh, darn!"

I hopped off the chair and knelt down to pick up the tarts, my face flushing with heat. But as I straightened up, I tripped and fell backwards toward the fireplace.

"Violet!" Tristan cried as I scrambled to grab the mantle. I managed to stop my fall, but my dress wasn't so lucky. The skirt grazed the merrily crackling fire… and a moment later, the beautiful sea-colored fabric was engulfed in flames.

I screamed, lurching away from the fireplace as the white-hot fire licked my legs, dimly aware that all eyes in the Great Hall were now on me. Suddenly, Cora appeared next to me with a pitcher of water. She flung it on me, dousing the flames.

"Are you okay, Miss?" she cried, her voice shaking.

I was too shocked to reply. I just stood there, damp and humiliated, my hair hanging in wet strands. A heavy silence settled over the room.

Then a murmur began, quickly growing to a roar as everyone pointed and stared. Emil made his way through the crowd, staring down at me as if I were a rat he'd found drowned in the toilet. Even Cora was looking at me with something close to fear in her eyes.

Grandfather made his way through the crowd. "What is it? What's happened?" His voice was gruff, and I heard the worry in his tone. "Violet, are you all right?"

But when his gaze fell on me, his expression quickly changed from worry to something else entirely—terror. After a moment, I realized why.

The soot had washed away, revealing the silver streak in my hair.

6

SPRITES

"V-Violet?"

Grandfather's voice trembled as he whispered my name.

That was what caused my blood to turn to ice. Not the fact that everyone was staring at me, at the strange silver streak in my hair. Not the way Cora was trembling, not the curious tilt of Tristan's head as he studied me, not the way Emil was glaring at me as if I were some beggar off the streets here to crash the party.

My own grandfather, the *king,* was terrified of me. And now all of Elsinore knew it.

I was a threat, in their eyes. A villain.

"Grandfather, I didn't...I don't..." I couldn't seem to find the words. I had no explanation for the silver streak in my hair, just as I had no explanation for the color of my eyes. But I hadn't done anything evil. Yet everyone, including the king, was looking at me as if I'd just cast the most wicked of spells.

I closed my eyes, but all I could see was flashes of my birthday last year. The storm with the blood-red lightning, the poor wounded foal caught up in debris, the screams as metal blades cut through the air, the stares of horror and whispers of *witch*.

It wasn't fair. I hadn't cursed anyone. If anything, *I* was the one who was cursed. My parents had been taken from me. My grandfather thought I was a danger to myself and others. But I had done nothing, *nothing* to warrant his suspicion. I didn't deserve to be called names like witch. What had I done that was so terrible? Saved a foal's life? I only wanted to help the poor creature. Was it the silver streak? My violet eyes? Did a few odd physical features automatically make me *wicked*?

It wasn't fair, it wasn't fair, it wasn't *fair*.

A hot seed of anger bloomed deep in my gut, blossoming and spreading up into my chest and racing up and down my arms and legs. I curled and uncurled my fingers, enjoying the warmth. The heat inside me grew more intense, and soon my damp hair and skin began to sizzle as the water evaporated.

"Violet? Are you okay?"

Tristan wheeled closer, reaching for me—but my skin was red-hot now, and though I felt no pain, I was certain that him touching me would be no different than touching poker that's been in the fire too long. I jerked my arm away, a strange pulse shimmered through the air...and Tristan went flying out of his wheelchair, landing in a heap on the marble floor.

"Tristan!" I cried in horror, but the sound was lost to the complete chaos that erupted. The crowd was screaming, shouting, shoving one another in their haste to get to the doors, to get as far away from the witch as possible. Cora ran to Tristan, kneeling down to help him sit up, and Grandfather was trembling like a leaf. Emil stared at me with a mix of fear and hatred that cut me to my core.

"I'll show you what we do to witches in Elsinore," he snarled, taking a step toward me.

But I barely heard what he'd said. My mind was suddenly filled with his treasonous words from last night. Grandfather trusted him, trusted his counsel, and Emil was plotting to undermine him all this time. He was plotting to take the throne from our family.

I imagined that magnificent creature in my dream, rising out of the ocean and sending waves crashing, and I felt the power rise up once more inside of me. Just before Emil reached me, I let out a scream that stopped him in his tracks.

The walls, the floor, everything shook, and then there was an almighty *smash* as every single window in the Great Hall shattered. Colorful shards of glass rained down on my party like confetti, and, as the people screamed in terror, I collapsed.

Some of the crowd, desperate to get away from me, began climbing out of the broken windows despite the fact that we were three floors up. I imagined them trapped on the ledges outside and let out a whimper.

"Tristan," I called weakly. "Tristan!"

I crawled toward him, and he reached out a hand toward me. But then Grandfather pulled him away, his eyes locked onto my face. "Stay away from him," he rasped.

The words cut through me like a knife. *I'm not going to hurt him,* I wanted to say. But the thing was, I already had. Tristan was lying in a heap on the floor because of me.

Fear and self-loathing twisted together deep in my stomach.

The royal guards spilled into the Great Hall, swords drawn. A groan died in my throat as I glanced from them, to Grandfather, to Cora, to Tristan…my dear, sweet cousin. He was the only person in the entire hall who didn't seem afraid—even though he was the only person I'd hurt.

So far.

My gaze moved to Emil. He was looking at the

royal guards, and I saw him nod. The tiniest nod, barely perceptible. An order. But they didn't obey Emil. They only obeyed the king.

Unless Emil's treasonous plot was already underway.

I got to my feet as the royal guards rushed toward me. Tristan saw them, too, and he tried to pull away from Grandfather. "Violet, wait," he said, but he was too late.

I lifted my arms high overhead, then brought them down hard, just like that creature in my dreams thrashing at the sea. And amazingly, impossibly, a nearly invisible current of power rushed through the air straight at the royal guards. They shouted as the wave I'd created knocked them off their feet, and when they landed on the floor, they lay stiff and frozen.

"Violet, what have you done?"

Grandfather's howl brought me back to my senses. I gasped for air, staring in horror at the unmoving guards. Had I truly done that? Even Emil had taken a step away from me now, his eyes narrowed. More guards were storming in, making it impossible for anyone to get out of the Great Hall—including me.

I couldn't stay here another minute. I needed them to get out of my way, but I didn't want to hurt them like I had the guards. I curled and uncurled my fingers, trying to think, when a soft, sweet voice in my head whispered:

It's simple, dear. Just summon something to take you away.

Summon what? But even as I had the thought, I was picturing a horse. Not just any horse.

Sprites.

No sooner had I pictured her then I heard the unmistakable sound of galloping hooves. "Impossible," I whispered, but a moment later, Sprites burst into the Great Hall. Fully grown now, storm cloud gray with that beautiful mane and tail streaking behind her just like the red lightning that was her namesake.

"Violet! Wait!"

Ignoring Tristan's plea, I climbed onto a chair and leaped onto Sprites' back. Threading my fingers through her blood-red mane, I held on tight as the magnificent horse rocketed out of the Great Hall. Guards and townspeople alike threw themselves out of our way, and I couldn't stop the thoughts flooding my mind at the sight of them on their knees.

You'll pay for calling me a witch.

You're right to fear me.

Kneel before your queen.

Sprites flew down the grand staircase and across the foyer. Outside, I inhaled the salty air and urged Sprites to run faster, faster, faster. Dark clouds were on the horizon over the sea, just like in my dreams.

They rolled in fast, quickly blocking the sun and casting a dark shadow over Crown Castle.

I tried to be good. This is their fault. All of them: the townspeople, Emil, Grandfather…they believe I'm evil, no matter what I do.

If they want evil, I'll show them evil.

The great stone wall grew closer, and my scowl deepened. As we passed through the entrance, I raised my right arm and threw it down, just as I had back in the Great Hall. A shimmering wave of power crashed down with it, causing the wall to shake. Sprites picked up speed, running down the beach, and I glanced over my shoulder in time to see several of the newer stones topple off the wall and land on the sand, each one causing an almighty *THUD*.

Good.

Turning, I leaned closer to Sprites and hugged her neck as he sprinted down the coast. Saltwater misted my face and clung to my dress, and my hair whipped wildly in the ocean breeze. With the castle growing distant behind me and nothing but sand and sea stretching out in front of me, I felt more than alive.

I felt free.

7

LOST AT SEA

Sprites and I traveled along the beach for what felt like hours. By the time she slowed her pace, the sky was beginning to darken. Gently, I urged her to turn around and head back to the castle.

The power I'd felt had receded slowly, and when Crown Castle came into view on the horizon, I no longer felt like a powerful queen. I felt cold and empty, like a bathtub drained of its chilly water. I felt like what I was: a sad, lost little girl.

What would happen when I returned? Would Grandfather lock me away in the forbidden wing? Or was he still too afraid of me to attempt any sort of punishment? The idea of my poor, sweet grandfather cowering from me caused my insides to writhe with guilt. I couldn't forget the way he'd trembled before me. The mighty King of Elsinore in his finest robes, crown flashing gold on his head, going to pieces in front of his people over an eleven-year-old girl with a silver streak in her hair.

It dawned on me for the first time that there would be no pretense of normal after this. After my last birthday, Grandfather had brushed aside the rumors and treated the windmill incident as an accident, a close call in which I was the victim. But this…there was no brushing it aside, no crafting another version of the story. Everyone had witnessed what I'd done. What would Grandfather do next?

I pictured Emil's beady eyes flashing with greed. He would turn this to his advantage, no doubt about it. He'd already convinced half the council that Grandfather was keeping some dark secret. Clearly, he had members of the royal guard on his side, too. What would he do, now that the princess—Elsinore's future queen—had all but confirmed the rumors that she was indeed a witch capable of terrible evil?

I was so lost in these thoughts, it took me a moment to realize something was terribly wrong with the castle.

"Whoa, girl," I whispered, digging my feet into Sprites' sides. The horse slowed obediently, and my breathing grew shallow as my brain began to comprehend what I was seeing.

The wall along the west side of the castle had completely collapsed. It looked as though a river had appeared out of nowhere, running from the sea straight into a gaping hole in the west wing.

My heart began to hammer wildly in my chest. I'd used that strange power to shake the wall, to topple a few stones from the top. But I'd looked back over my shoulder as Sprites and I had raced away, and the wall still stood. I hadn't done this.

Had I?

But if I hadn't, who had?

The tide was high, and that, too, was not right. Through the silvery clouds overhead, I could just make out the moon against the darkening sky—the barest sliver of a crescent. What could have caused this flood? A hurricane? No, surely not. I couldn't have traveled outside the reach of a hurricane in such a short span of time. Even Sprites wasn't that fast.

I guided Sprites off the beach and onto the grounds, then climbed off as quickly as I could. After giving her a hasty kiss on the nose, I left her grazing the grass and sprinted into the castle as fast as my legs could carry me.

My footsteps echoed around the foyer as I walked slowly across the marble floor. "Grandfather?" I called, the word bouncing off the walls. But there was no response.

The knot in my stomach tightened as I made my way toward the ballroom. I stopped short in the entrance, hot tears of shame flooding my eyes at the sight before me. The hall was completely empty and in total disarray: chairs overturned, food everywhere, gleaming shards of glass littering the marble floor. Wind howled through the windows, and the fireplace that had been crackling so merrily earlier had long gone cold.

Turning, I walked away from the Great Hall and wiped the tears from my eyes. The castle had never felt so empty. Had they all fled, leaving me behind? Even Tristan?

Could I blame them if they had?

Suddenly, I remembered the giant hole in the west wing. Of course! Everyone was probably there, inspecting the damage. I picked up my pace, heading for the stairs again. Portraits of past kings and queens stared stony-faced at me as I ran down hallway after hallway. I could practically feel their disapproval.

For once, I was grateful for Grandfather's overprotectiveness. He'd locked the west wing up tight two years ago, which meant that no one had been there when whatever had happened to cause the flood happened. At least, that was what I told myself over and over again. But the knot in my stomach was worse than ever, and an all too familiar feeling of dread was creeping up my spine.

I'd felt this way the day my parents never came home, long before the storm had hit. Sometimes, when something big and awful loomed on the horizon, you just *knew*.

I passed the library and the sitting room, my heart skipping a beat as I pictured Emil lunging through the double doors, sword drawn. But the castle was as quiet as a graveyard.

At last, the great double doors to the west wing came into view. The sight of them open, the padlock Grandfather had affixed two years ago hanging loose, was somehow even stranger than the windowless Great Hall or the river running through the broken wall.

I slowed down as I approached the doors. That sensation of dread was stronger than ever, slithering up my spine and winding around my rib cage like cold, damp vines. Slipping between the doors, I stared around at the west wing for the first time in over two years.

This had been Mother's favorite wing of the castle because of the views. The wide corridor stretched out in front of me, but my eyes were drawn to the right wall. It was floor-to-ceiling windows, revealing a view of the broken wall, the flooded grounds, and the ocean beyond that took my breath away.

I walked down the hall, wishing I had a cloak, or maybe my fluffy bathrobe. The air in the corridor was stale but cool, and a light sheen of mist from the sea still covered my skin and my dress. As I neared the first of the smaller hallways, familiar voices reached my ears. I turned the corner and went weak with relief at the sight of Cora, Sirena, and Grandfather. Emil was there, too, but at the moment, I didn't care.

Cora saw me first. Her eyes went wide with alarm, and for a moment, I froze. *I shouldn't have come back. They're all terrified of me, and rightly so.* Then she bustled towards me and swept me up in a hug, spinning me around so that my back was to Grandfather and Sirena, who were deep in conversation and hadn't noticed me yet.

"Oh, Miss Violet," she whispered, squeezing me so tight I gasped. "I am so, so glad you're okay. We were all so worried."

Fresh tears sprang to my eyes as I hugged her back. "I'm sorry for what I did," I choked out. "I didn't mean to…I don't know how…"

"I know, I know," she said, finally releasing me. "Come now, love, let me make you some hot chocolate. You look chilled to the bone."

"But I want to talk to Grandfather." Even as I tried to turn around, Cora gripped my arm tighter and tugged me farther away. Frowning, I planted my feet firmly and wrestled out of her grasp. "Cora! I know he's angry, but I want to talk to him!"

"No, love, that's not it—"

Cora made another grab for me, but I was too quick for her. Ducking around my maid, I ran down the hallway. Grandfather and Sirena looked up, both of them moving in unison as if to block something from my view.

"Violet," Grandfather said softly. The fear from earlier was gone, but there was a trepidation on his wrinkled face that I didn't like one bit. "Go with Cora, please. I'll come speak with you soon."

"Why? What's going on? I..." The words died on my lips.

Behind Grandfather and Sirena, one of the wall panels was slightly ajar. There was no doorknob, nothing to indicate it could be opened, and for a moment I felt a little thrill of delight at the idea of a hidden door leading to a secret passage.

Then I remembered Tristan's present.

It has nothing to do with hiding in a secret passage from that weasel, he'd said with that mysterious smile. *Well, it has nothing to do with that weasel, anyway.*

Tristan had been taking me to the west wing. This was my present: a brand-new secret passage.

As if in a dream, I moved slowly until I could see inside. The light was dim, but I could just make out what lay on the damp ground.

An overturned wheelchair, broken and busted.

The world tilted. I fell to my knees, vaguely aware

of the others rushing to help me. Their voices sounded far away and murky, as if I was deep underwater. The image was burned into my mind: the wheelchair on its side, one wheel lazily spinning, the other jutting out at an awkward angle. The torn leather chair. The armrest, snapped in half. The drip-drip-drip of water from the ceiling. I had always loved the smell of saltwater, but now it made my stomach churn.

"You did this."

Emil's cruel words broke through my trance. I blinked and gazed up into his sneering face.

"You and your tantrum, your—your unnatural power—"

"Stop," Grandfather said in a low voice, but Emil did not stop.

"You attack your own party guests and flee the castle," he said, sneering at me. "Then a great hole is ripped in the west wall just as a massive wave surges up, flooding this passage? That is not an act of nature. That is an act of *magic*. Your own cousin was here, and you pulled him out to sea and *drowned him*—"

"Enough!" Grandfather thundered, and Emil cowered back against the wall. "Your counsel is no longer needed, Emil. You are dismissed."

"But my lord, I only—"

"You are *dismissed*!"

Grandfather stood up straight and tall, his booming voice echoing around the small corridor. The blood drained from Emil's face.

"You'll regret this, *sir*," he spat in such a vehement tone, even Grandfather looked taken aback. "I know what you're hiding. About that girl. About the curse. Because of your foolish deal, Lydian was…" His voice trembled on my mother's name. I stared at Emil, flabbergasted as he caught himself. "You've put all of Elsinore at risk just to keep that little witch safe—"

With a roar, Grandfather struck Emil hard with the back of his hand. Emil reeled back with a cry of pain, hand to his jaw. Already, I could see swelling appear on his cheek. With a final, hateful glare, Emil scurried back out into the main hallway and slipped away like a rat.

Grandfather's shoulders slumped as if all the fight had drained out of him. I realized I was shaking. What had he meant about my mother?

Sirena grabbed my hands in her large, warm ones, squeezing them gently. "Don't you listen to him now, love," she whispered. "We know this wasn't your doing."

"Exactly," Grandfather said. "It was mine."

Shocked, I looked up at him. Sirena and Cora did as well, wearing identical expressions of surprise.

"My lord?" Sirena asked.

Grandfather sighed heavily, his shoulders sagging. "I knew this was coming. This is why I locked the west wing. This is why I ordered the wall built. This is why for the last two years I've done everything I could to protect Violet and Tristan…but it wasn't enough. I didn't do enough. I failed. And now Tristan…my dear grandson is lost to the sea, just like…"

His voice broke, and he began to sob. Sirena moved towards him, throwing an arm around him and guiding him to the hallway. I heard her murmuring soothing words that I could just barely make out.

"You've sent out a search party, my lord. They're looking as we speak. Don't give up hope."

Numbness spread over me. Grandfather blamed himself for not doing enough to keep me locked up. But we both knew this was my fault. Somehow, I had caused this flood. As much as I hated him, I knew Emil had been right.

I had as good as killed Tristan myself.

"Violet, dear," Cora said, resting her hand on her shoulder. I could feel that she was shaking, and I knew she was just trying to hold herself together for my sake. "Come now, a nice cup of tea and you'll—"

"I don't want tea!" I screamed, throwing her hand off. She stumbled back, her bright eyes wide with fear, and guilt flooded through me. Bursting into tears, I raced away from the awful sight of the broken wheelchair, out of the west wing, and all the way to my room.

As I pushed my door open, through the blur of tears, I saw something flutter to the carpet. A folded piece of paper. Blinking and hiccupping, I kneeled down to pick it up. I shrieked with joy, covering my mouth at the sight of Tristan's familiar handwriting.

For Violet's eyes only.

I knew before I unfolded it that the paper would appear blank. Hastily wiping my eyes, I hurried over to the candle on my bedside table. Tristan and I had learned long ago how to write letters to one another in invisible ink. All we had to do was steal the odd lemon from the kitchen without Sirena noticing.

My hands shook as I carefully held the paper over the tiny flame. When had Tristan slipped this into my doorjamb? It couldn't have been before the party; he'd already been in the Great Hall when I'd arrived. So, he must have written this after I'd fled, but before…before the flood.

At last, words began to appear on the paper, faint but readable. My pulse thrummed as I read Tristan's note.

Dear Violet,

I know you didn't mean to hurt me at the party, and I made everything worse by trying to help you. I should have told you this a year ago, but I was afraid it would frighten you.

I saw what happened with the windmill.

Whatever I had been expecting, it wasn't this. I

66

sank down onto my bed, my hand trembling so hard I could barely read Tristan's script.

I was watching the storm out of my window before your party, admiring the sprites. Then I saw you running across the grounds toward that horse and her trapped foal. I saw the townspeople staring. I saw you rescue the foal, and then the blades came off the windmill...

I was so scared, Violet. I thought you were about to die right in front of my eyes.

Instead, you did something AMAZING.

You stood there and stared at the blades flying through the air. You lifted your arms up, and then you threw them down and...this part's hard to describe. It was like you had thrown a giant invisible boulder into the sea and the water rippled out, only it was the air rippling, and it sent the blades flying back with such force I couldn't believe it. They vanished somewhere in the treetops. I imagine they're still there.

Then you collapsed.

That's what everyone saw. I didn't tell you because you were so upset about all the witch rumors, and I didn't know how you'd react if I told you that I thought you actually might have some sort of...power.

Instead, I started researching. I was hoping to find some answers first, and then I was going to tell you, I swear. But none of that matters. I should have told you right away. I should have warned you.

Maybe what happened at the party today wouldn't have happened. Maybe you would have been able to control it.

Because what you did to the guards? That was the same thing you did to the windmill. That's why everyone was so frightened. It was happening again.

Please, please forgive me for not telling you sooner. You're not alone, Violet. We'll figure out what this means together. I've learned a lot from that book I showed you, and I think you should read it, too.

Anyway, I hope my birthday present will make this day a little bit better. You were right about it being in the west wing. I found a secret passage that leads to the ocean! It goes UNDER the wall! You can still visit the ocean whenever you want, no matter how tall Grandfather builds the wall. When you get this, meet me in the west wing and I'll show you. I'll wait there.

Love,

Tristan

His words blurred, and I crumpled the note in my fist with a groan. All this time, I had no idea anyone else had witnessed what happened with the windmill. Tristan had seen it all. He knew I had powers even before I did. Only while everyone else had seen me as a witch, Tristan had seen me as a hero.

Dear, sweet Tristan had wanted to help me. He'd even found a way to give me the ocean…and now I'd lost him to it forever.

Until this moment, the reality of it hadn't sunk in. I would never see my cousin again. Throwing myself onto my bed, I sobbed into my pillow.

THUD.

THUD.

THUD.

Outside, Grandfather's men were back at work on the wall, despite the late hour. Grandfather would no doubt close up that secret passage and lock up the west wing once more. He would build that wall to the moon if that was what it took to keep me locked in, keep me safe. Keep everyone else safe from me.

But I wasn't safe. I was cursed. I had killed my cousin.

Maybe I truly was a witch, after all.

I wept until I had no tears left, eventually drifting off to sleep to the sounds of stones piling higher and higher.

8

HYDRA

Once more, my dreams were filled with water. Only now, they were murky, dim and inhospitable.

I swam against the current, occasionally spotting a shape up ahead—a hand, maybe, or a foot—and I kept reaching for them, swimming faster and faster, but the current was determined to keep us apart.

I awoke with a start, gasping for air. My room was dark. Too dark.

Something was wrong.

Even during a new moon, my room didn't get this pitch-black in the middle of the night. There was starlight, and even on cloudy nights, the reflection of the clouds off the ocean was enough to provide a dim light through my window.

And that wasn't the only thing. The air was far too still. I always slept with the windows open—Cora had long given up on trying to close them before I went to sleep. I loved the breeze and the way it would carry in that salty, briny smell. But now, there was no breeze. The air was stale and warm, and lying under my heavy blankets, I felt like I was in a coffin.

I threw the blankets off and ran to the window, desperate to breathe in the fresh night air. But when I threw aside the curtains, it took me a moment to realize what I was looking at.

Stones.

"Impossible," I whispered, blinking rapidly. But the stones remained, boarding up my window.

With a cry, I raced to my door and threw it open— and ran smack into another stone wall.

I landed hard on my back, disoriented and terrified. No, this couldn't be. Grandfather wouldn't wall me up inside my room. Not literally. How would Cora bring me food? How would she teach my lessons? Surely, Grandfather didn't mean for…he didn't intend for me to stay in here *forever*…

I was hyperventilating now. This must be a nightmare. I pinched myself on the arm so hard I knew it would leave a bruise, but I didn't wake up.

Which meant this was real. This was happening.

My lungs were going to burst. Dizzy, I tried to get to my feet but swayed and bumped into the wall. A faint flicker of green caught my eye, and I focused on it. Light! That was *light*. But where was it coming from?

I took a deep breath in, then let it out, willing my heartbeat to slow as I gazed around. Was it my imagination, or was the flicker getting brighter? And *spreading*?

Soon, all four walls of my room shimmered with that otherworldly green glow. But I still couldn't find the source of the light. I made my way along the wall, tracing my fingers along the wallpaper. It was slick and wet with dew. I frowned. What was going on?

"Hello, Violet."

Even as I whirled around, I recognized that soft, sweet voice. It was the same voice I'd heard in my mind at the party. *It's simple, dear. Just summon something to take you away.*

In all the madness that had followed, I'd nearly forgotten about the voice and whom it could have belonged to. But now I didn't have to wonder, because she was standing in the middle of my bedroom.

She was…I wasn't sure if *beautiful* was the right word. *Striking.* Sirena was fond of saying that about unusual-looking people, and I had never been quite sure what she meant. But now I fully understand. This woman was *striking*.

Her dark hair billowed around her head as if she were underwater. Her skin was a shiny walnut-brown, and her eyes were the color of rich Ember. She wore a gold dress that seemed to be one long, slippery stretch of fabric that wound around her arms, shoulders, and waist in a complicated way. Dimly, I remembered the dress I'd been so proud to wear to my party, with its iridescent fabric. Compared to this woman's dress, mine was childish. Her dress seemed to be woven from magic itself.

I swallowed hard. "W-who are you?" I whispered.

She smiled, baring white teeth that shone bright despite the dimness of the room.

"You may call me Hydra."

Hydra. I couldn't stop staring at her. I felt as though I was under a spell. "Are you a witch?"

The words tumbled out before I could stop them, and I wanted to kick myself. Because of all people, I should have known better. Didn't I hate it when people assumed I was a witch, simply because of my purple eyes? But Hydra didn't appear annoyed in the slightest. If anything, her lips quirked up in amusement.

"I have extraordinary powers," she said simply. "Whatever people might call me is only out of fear of those powers."

The memory of the power I had wielded hours ago flooded through me. I felt the thrill of what I'd

73

done, slashing my arms in the air and knocking down the king's guards as if they were no more than chess pieces. For the first time, rather than shame, I felt pride. I felt *strong*.

"What sort of powers do you have?" I asked eagerly.

Hydra smiled fully now. "Would you like a demonstration?" she asked.

I hesitated.

But what else was there to say? How could I possibly say no to a demonstration of real, actual magic?

"Yes."

Hydra's eyes flickered, and I waited for her to wave her arms or utter some incantation. But she did neither. After a few seconds, I opened my mouth to ask what she planned on doing…and that was when I realized my slippers were soaking wet.

Looking down, I saw dark, salty water pooling around me. My entire room was filling up with water. And *fast*.

Seawater rushed in from some unseen opening—the window and the door were boarded up so tightly—and terror seized me like a vice.

"What are you doing?" I cried, my voice high-pitched with fear. Hydra merely watched me as I thrashed in the water, trying to make my way toward the door even though I knew it was locked.

Then the water swept me up and I was submerged.

I kicked and flailed, my heart hammering so hard I thought it might burst right out of my chest and swim away. I was going to die.

I was going to drown just like my parents. Just like Tristan.

My head grazed the gilded ceiling, and my lungs began to burn. I couldn't hold my breath much longer. I stared through the water, locking eyes with Hydra, mentally pleading with her to spare me.

A smile curved her lips. Then she opened her mouth and said, "*Breathe.*"

Shocked by the sound of her voice underwater, I released the air in my lungs in a long stream of bubbles. Then I inhaled. And again.

I could breathe. I could breathe *underwater.*

I let out a strangled laugh of relief. Now that my pulse was beginning to slow, I could see that my entire chamber was transformed. I could still see the hardwood floors, the walls, the ceiling, but it was as if Hydra had summoned all of the most beautiful parts of the ocean right here for me. Sparkling orange starfish, shiny green seaweed, and goldfish that glittered like the coins Grandfather kept stored away in the vault danced and twirled all around me.

I let out a breathless little laugh as a starfish bopped me on the nose. Then I dove down to the floor, running my fingers over the slick, algae-covered rocks that had appeared. A hermit crab peered up at me curiously, and I giggled again.

Kicking off of the floor, I soared back up to the ceiling. Swimming felt so easy, so natural. Hydra watched me, her smile growing wider and wider at my joy.

And then, as quickly as it had appeared, the water began to subside. My head broke the surface as my own personal ocean lowered me gently back to the floor, and soon it was gone.

I stood there by my bed, sopping wet and thrilled to the core. "That was *amazing*!"

"I'm glad you thought so," Hydra replied. "Violet, you have the power to summon the ocean as well. As a matter of fact, you have the power to do whatever you'd like. You proved that today, didn't you?"

I swallowed hard. "Yes. But I—I can't control it like you can. It…it scares me."

"You will learn," Hydra said, as if it had already been decided. She cast a derisive glance at the stones sealing up my window. "This future you're facing, being made a prisoner in your own home by a cowardly king who fears you—that does not have to be your fate."

The word *cowardly* sent a ripple of anger and defensiveness through me. Grandfather was not a coward. He was a brave man, a good king.

Then why is he locking you up? I winced at the

thought. But Hydra was right. Grandfather was imprisoning me. He feared me.

Hydra made a sympathetic *tsk-tsk* sound with her tongue. "Oh, darling. I know the king means well, I truly do. But he simply does not understand you. He's trying to protect you from your own powers!" She moved closer, her eyes locking onto mine, never blinking once. "*You* are the one with all the power here! Not the king! He needs you—this kingdom needs you! You do not need protecting—you need *freedom*."

Her words rang in my mind like peal of the kitchen bells calling me to dinner. Hydra was right. Why would a girl with the power to take down the king's guards with a simple wave of her arms need protecting?

My shoulders straightened, and I lifted my chin.

Hydra looked pleased. "It's everyone else who needs protecting," she went on. "Look at what happened when you were unjustly driven from your own castle, your home. You weren't there to protect your poor cousin."

The word was a knife in my heart. My eyes burned with tears. *Tristan.*

"And now…" Sighing, Hydra took a step back and raised her arms. "Well, now see for yourself what has happened to that poor unfortunate soul."

A massive, shimmering bubble appeared between

us. Blinking, I gazed at it in awe as an image came into focus. It appeared to be a cage, rusty and covered with algae. And inside, curled up in the corner, was a person. A boy.

"Tristan!" I cried, moving closer. But as I reached for him, the image blurred and faded, and soon the cage was replaced with a sunken ship. "I don't understand—has he been kidnapped? Was it pirates? Is he on that ship? But it's at the bottom of the sea, how can he breathe?"

Hydra jabbed the bubble with her long, pointed fingernail, and the bubble vanished with a light *pop*! Hydra watched me, her expression difficult to read.

A swell of emotions rose inside me, conflicting feelings that sloshed against one another: joy, fear, rage, confusion.

Tristan was alive.

But he was a prisoner.

A prisoner in the ocean.

"Who took him?" I demanded, my voice a shaky rasp.

Hydra was silent for a long moment, regarding me. Then she sighed.

"The same evil that took your parents, I'm afraid."

My parents.

Heat spread through me as the meaning of her words sank in. Their deaths hadn't been an accident. All this time, I thought they'd been lost in a storm, but no—someone was responsible. The same someone who'd taken my cousin.

And that someone was going to pay.

"I'm going to rescue him," I told Hydra, and the hardness in my voice surprised even me. "And then I'm going to destroy whoever did this."

Hydra looked pleased at my fury. "Spoken like a true queen," she said, and I felt a rush of pleasure at her words. "Your grandfather has many secrets locked away in the west wing. The passage your cousin discovered was just one. So sweet of him to turn it into a surprise birthday present for you," she added, and my throat tightened as I imagined Tristan waiting at the secret passage, no doubt so pleased with himself. "Speaking of, I know I wasn't invited to the party, but I have a little surprise of my own for you. Yet another little treasure the king has kept hidden from you."

I watched as Hydra conjured the bubble again, hoping for another glimpse of Tristan. Instead, I saw a silvery oyster shell. It was half-open, just wide enough for me to glimpse the perfect, white pearl at the center.

"That's in the west wing?" I asked, entranced. The pearl seemed to glow before my eyes.

"Indeed," Hydra replied. "And it's all you need to save your cousin."

Before I could respond, Hydra and the bubble

had vanished. "Wait!" I cried, lunging forward—and suddenly, I was sitting up straight in bed.

Panting as if I'd just sprinted down the beach, I threw off my blankets and stared around wildly. My curtains fluttered in the breeze, the night sky visible beyond.

Disappointment flooded me. It had all been a dream. I had actually let myself believe Tristan was alive, and now I felt the crushing weight of his death all over again.

Slipping out of bed, I headed to the window. The wall was already blocking some of my view of the ocean. I grasped the windowsill and squeezed until my knuckles turned white, furious with Grandfather, and furious with myself. Did I really want my poor cousin trapped as a prisoner at the bottom of the ocean? Was that really better than death?

If there was a chance of rescue, then yes.

My shoulders slumped. When I turned to go back to bed, I saw a gold of something shiny poking out from under my pillow. Pulling it out, I gazed at it in amazement.

A compact mirror, shaped like a gold shell. Engraved onto the back of the compact, it read in fine script "You are a world away". I flipped it open and gasped.

"Tristan!"

I could see him in the mirror, just as he'd appeared

in Hydra's bubble! He was curled up in that awful cage. He shifted slightly, his head lifting, and my spirits soared because he must have heard me, maybe he could tell me how to find him—

And then the image faded, and I found myself staring at my own shocked reflection.

"Tristan? Tristan!" I said desperately, shaking the compact. I closed it and opened it, hoping for another glimpse of him, but the mirror would only show me my pale, haunted face.

For a moment, my disappointment was a weight that threatened to crush me. Then I snapped the compact closed and squeezed it tight.

This was proof that last night hadn't been a dream. Hydra had really been here in my room.

And Tristan really was alive!

9

MAP QUEST

I knew I couldn't waste a single moment. Not with my cousin trapped down at the bottom of the ocean, the prisoner of some mysterious foe.

Throwing my riding cloak on top of my nightgown, I slipped out of my bedchambers and headed straight for the west wing.

The pearl. *It's all you need to save your cousin,* Hydra had said. I didn't have a clue how a pearl could possibly help me, but right now, it was all I had to go on. I would turn the entire west wing upside-down until I found it.

I flew down the hall as silent as a ghost, past portrait after portrait of regal scowls and disapproving glares.

Suddenly, a distant *shuffle-shuffle* sound reached my ears, and I stumbled to a halt, nearly upsetting the suit of armor standing guard at the end of the hall. The sound was coming from the end of the corridor I'd just passed.

Someone else was awake. Sirena, maybe? It wouldn't be the first time. Tristan and I knew from past midnight excursions that the chef was sometimes up at late hours. She could have been checking on Grandfather, I reasoned. And then a far worse thought hit me.

Emil. I pictured the expression on his face earlier, that look of pure loathing and disgust. He obeyed Grandfather's orders, of course, but what would he do to me if the king weren't around to stop him?

Let him try, a voice hissed in my head. *Then show him what* real *power looks like.*

Straightening my spine, I turned and stared down the dark hall. The shuffling grew louder, and I clenched my fists, prepared for a fight.

When Flotsam and Jetsam burst out of the corridor, skidding on the marble floor as they swiveled to face me, I let out a yelp of surprise that was part-laugh. Then I clamped my hand over my mouth, glancing around.

The pups scampered over, tails wagging ferociously, and I knelt down to give them both kisses and scratches behind the ears. That urge to fight, wherever it had come from, drained out of me. Now I felt small and weak and scared. A young girl who'd just lost her cousin, wandering around a cold, dark castle. I gathered Flotsam and Jetsam up in my arms and hugged them close, grateful for their companionship.

Feeling slightly better, I stood and made my way downstairs to the first floor, and then to the west wing, my beloved pups at my side. They seemed to know that this was a secret errand; I could have sworn Flotsam was making an effort to keep his nails from clacking on the marble, and Jetsam didn't let out so much as a whine when I pulled open the doors to the west wing and a mouse scurried out, darting in a zigzag until it found refuge behind the statue of a portly bishop.

I closed the doors to the west wing carefully behind us, and we set off down the wide hall. At night, it felt like a different place entirely; no sunlight streaming in through those massive windows, just darkness punctuated with pinpricks of starlight. It dawned on me that searching the west wing in the pitch-black for a very small item was not going to be the easiest task. Especially considering I had no idea where to even begin looking.

I'd been walking for nearly a full minute before I realized my footsteps weren't the only ones I heard echoing off the stone walls.

I froze, and so did Flotsam and Jetsam. The other footsteps stopped a second later. The hall was silent, but it wasn't the calm quiet of night. It was the sort of silence that was laced with tension, a rubber band pulled as tight as it could go before it snapped.

Someone was following me.

As noiselessly as possible, I glanced over my shoulder. I couldn't see anyone, but the moonlight cast so many shadows across the hall—my stalker could have been hiding in any of them.

I began walking again, slowly, quietly. For a few seconds, I heard nothing. Then it started again, the soft yet unmistakable sound of feet shuffling across the floor behind me. It wasn't Sirena, or Cora, or Grandfather, I knew—they wouldn't sneak up on me. They would confront me. I pictured the reedy-looking council member prowling the library, searching for whoever had been spying on the secret meeting and silently cursed my own stupidity. I had crept right past the library *and* the sitting room where Emil had been plotting treason. Of course, he would have posted a lookout there tonight. I shuddered as I realized I must have walked right past them on my way to the west wing. And now, I was alone with that person in the west wing, without anyone around to hear me cry for help.

Panic gripped me, and I ran.

Flotsam and Jetsam scurried along on either side

of me. I could hear the footsteps pounding loud behind me—whoever it was, they were no longer trying to keep quiet.

I hurtled around the next corridor I came to, my eyes darting frantically around, seeking for an open door. I spotted one up ahead, and my heart soared—but then I realized what it was, and I almost groaned.

The secret passage Tristan had found. The one that had flooded, pulling him out to sea.

The footsteps behind me were gaining fast. Any moment, my stalker would round the corner and spot me. I had to hide before he could see me, and this was my only option.

I slipped into the passage and fell still, listening over the sound of my rapid heartbeat for the footsteps. They'd slowed, the stalker now taking his time, trying to work out where I'd gone. But he was moving closer. He would almost certainly peek in the passage.

I had to go deeper inside.

Bracing myself for the sight of Tristan's broken wheelchair, I turned around. But it was gone. I let out a soft sigh as I hurried into the darkness, half-relieved, half-disappointed. Perhaps Grandfather had had one of his men take it in for repairs. Or, I realized with a sharp drop in my stomach, perhaps he'd had it thrown out, believing Tristan to be dead.

But Tristan wasn't dead. And he was coming

home. I would see to that.

The darkness of the passage swallowed me. It smelled of seawater, and a few cold, fat drops landed on my head, sliding down my neck and sending goosebumps down my arms. It was far darker in here than in the west wing's main hall, no soft light from the moon and stars, and my eyes couldn't seem to adjust. The blackness stretched out in front of me like an endless void.

I scooped up Flotsam and Jetsam and turned to face the entrance again. I could barely see the sliver of dim light near the entrance. As I watched, the sliver widened…and the silhouette of a lanky man filled the space.

The reedy-looking man. What was his name? It sounded like *rotten*…Rodden, that was it. I shuddered hard, squeezing my pups close and willing him not to step inside. If I moved now, he would almost certainly hear me—and I had no idea how long this passage ran. He would surely catch me before I reached the end. My only hope was to stay absolutely still and silent and hope he moved on to search the rest of the west wing.

He took one step forward, and then another. I wanted desperately to squeeze my eyes closed, but I couldn't look away.

One more step, and then he paused. I held my breath, watching as he slowly turned back to the entrance…and then Jetsam let out the softest, faintest whimper.

Rodden looked sharply down the hall, and I bit back a scream. I was too far back for him to see me, wasn't I? Should I move back farther, or would he spot the movement? I clutched Flotsam and Jetsam's warm, furry bodies close as I waited breathlessly to see what he would do first.

But before either of us could move, the distant sound of a door slamming made us both jump.

Rodden whirled around and flew out of the passage. I sank to my knees, listening to the sound of his footsteps fading and nearly weeping with relief. I kissed Flotsam and Jetsam each on top of the head before setting them down and getting to my feet.

"We still have to be quiet, now," I whispered to Flotsam. I could barely see the sparkle of his dark eyes in the passage, the glint of his white teeth bared in a doggie grin. Jetsam trotted deeper into the passage, sniffing loudly the way he did when he roamed the castle grounds on the hunt for squirrels. "Jetsam? Don't go too far!"

A moment later, he came trotting back to me. I was startled to realize he had something flat and yellow clamped gently between his teeth.

"What's this?" I wondered, taking it from him. It was parchment paper, slightly damp but rolled up and tied with a piece of seaweed. Quickly, I untied the seaweed and unfurled the paper. I held it close to my eyes, waiting for them to adjust. My heart skipped a beat when I realized what I was looking at.

A *map.*

For the briefest of moments, I imagined pirates in black masks and carrying swords, rushing down the secret passage and wrestling Tristan from his wheelchair. My stomach lurched at the thought of how frightened he must have been…then I saw this was no treasure map in my hands.

It was a map of the west wing!

I stared at the neatly labeled rooms, various bedchambers for guests, chapels and oratories, cabinets and boudoirs…and there, in the room labeled "Solar," was a sketch of an oyster shell.

Now my heart was hammering for an entirely different reason. This *was* a treasure map, at least for me! For a split second, in the dark, I thought I caught the flash of Hydra's smile.

"Thank you," I whispered, and then I hurried out of the passage with my pups.

The Solar was—or had been—a private suite of rooms just for the royal family. A place where servants and cabinet members weren't allowed, where kings and queens, lords and ladies, princes and princesses could relax for a bit and not worry about acting so…well, royal. If I strained my mind, I could dredge up a few memories of sitting in front of a crackling fireplace doing puzzles with my father or curling up on the sofa with a book while my mother knitted gloves and scarves for the gardeners.

I made my way through the winding corridors, moving quickly but quietly, listening for any signs of Rodden. And whoever had slammed the door, I reminded myself. I need to be stealthy.

No sooner did the thought enter my mind than I tripped and bumped into a decorative shield hanging on the wall. I leaped back, catching a glimpse of the Kronborg coat of arms painted onto the metal surface before it hit the marble floor with an almighty *CRASH.*

"Run!" I hissed to my pups, sprinting down the corridor. We were so close to the Solar, I just had to get there before Rodden or his companion spotted me.

"This way!" came the distant shout of a man's voice, but I couldn't even tell from which direction it had come. I put on a burst of speed as I hurtled around yet another corner. There, I could see the brass double doors! I ran flat-out, not even caring if they could hear my pounding footsteps. When I reached the doors, I shoved them open, waiting just long enough for my pups to scoot inside, then slammed the doors closed.

"Please still be here, please still be here..." I muttered, feeling around the door frame. "Yes!" I pulled out the thick, silver rod and slid it between the door handles. I gave the handles a tug to test it out the lock. The doors didn't even budge.

I placed a finger to my lips, and Flotsam and Jetsam both sat very still. We listened hard, but I didn't hear anything on the other side of the door. No footsteps, no voices.

At least, I heaved a sigh of relief and turned to look at the room properly for the first time.

The main suite of the Solar had one large window, and the moonlight illuminated what at first glance looked like a labyrinth. I blinked, standing uncertainly in the doorway. Then I realized what I was looking at.

Stacks upon stacks of books.

I stepped inside cautiously, making my way through the maze of books. My parents' books, I knew—they were both avid readers and writers—and slipped in here and there among the leather-bound encyclopedias and memoirs were journals no doubt filled with their own handwriting.

I knew I needed to focus on finding the pearl, but the urge to slide a notebook from the stacks and flip through pages of my father's neat print or my mother's looping cursive was overwhelming. Tears pricked the corners of my eyes as I pored over their writing. The words blurred in front of me, but I didn't care. For the first time in two years, I felt close to my parents again.

Then I caught sight of a green bottle with a letter neatly rolled up inside. My eyes went straight to one of the words scrawled on the letter. *Violet.*

Hastily, I pulled the cork out of the bottle and tipped the letter into my palm. Wiping my eyes, I began to read.

Your Royal Highness,

I realize it is quite out of the ordinary for the daughter of the King of Elsinore to write to you, but these are extraordinary circumstances. Our kingdoms have always been the greatest of allies, and I am hoping that will earn me forgiveness for my impertinence.

I have recently learned of the pact you and my father made in order to defeat the Dark Ones. While I appreciate the difficult decision you were facing and the complexity of the curse, I must protest at the inclusion of my daughter.

My Violet is barely nine years old. To tie her fate into this curse is nothing short of cruel. She must be allowed to choose her own path, to make her own choices. To do anything less would make us no better than the Dark Ones themselves.

I have spoken to my father on this matter, and we do not see eye to eye. Therefore, I am hoping you will listen and show mercy on my daughter. I humbly request a meeting at your earliest convenience.

Yours respectfully,
Lydian

I stared at the letter, dumbfounded. There was no address, no name. But slowly, I realized who the letter's intended recipient must have been. *Your Royal Highness.* Another king, but not Grandfather. The king with whom he'd joined forces with to defeat the Dark Ones.

Poseidon.

My throat tightened. *To tie her fate into this curse is nothing short of cruel.* Then I remembered the words Emil had hissed so angrily when Grandfather had dismissed him.

I know what you're hiding. About that girl. About the curse. Because of your foolish deal, Lydian was...

Killed. I pressed my lips together. That must have been what Emil was going to say.

My pulse was racing nearly as fast as it had been when Rodden had cornered me in the secret passage. I squeezed my eyes closed. I felt as though I had most of the puzzle pieces in front of me, and I just needed to fit them into the right spots.

Grandfather and Poseidon had made a pact to defeat the Dark Ones. A pact that involved the curse...and me. My mother found out and implored Grandfather to leave me out of it, but—my stomach churned unpleasantly—he must have refused. So, Mother had written to Poseidon.

Only he must not have received the letter, because here it was, locked up in the west wing.

With a start, I remembered overhearing Mother and Grandfather arguing the day before she died. I hadn't been able to make out the words. Tristan and I had been playing hide-and-seek on the castle grounds and saw them way out on the beach. Grandfather had been waving something angrily, and my mother appeared to be pleading with him…

My eyes fell on the green bottle. *That* was what Grandfather had gripped so tightly in his hands, arms flailing in fury. He must have caught Mother trying to send her message to Poseidon. He kept the letter.

The next day, my parents had gone out on their boat and capsized during a storm.

"No," I whispered as the truth began to dawn on me. But there was no point denying it. My parents hadn't been off on some leisurely boat ride. Since Grandfather had prevented Mother from sending Poseidon her letter, she was determined to speak to him in person.

Only she and my father died before they could find him.

I stood there, feeling as though I'd been ripped in half. One part of me felt a deep, powerful sympathy for Grandfather. No wonder his grief was so unending. He blamed himself for my parents' deaths. If he'd relented to my mother's request, or at the very least, allowed her to send her letter to Poseidon, she wouldn't have gone sailing the day of the storm.

Another part of me seethed with new rage. Because I couldn't help but blame Grandfather for my parents' deaths, too.

A sandpaper tongue licked my ankle, bringing me back to the present. I leaned down to scratch Flotsam behind the ear before rolling up Mother's letter and placing it back in the bottle. It felt as though a dozen new questions were blooming in my mind with every second that passed, but I didn't have time for that right now. I needed to focus.

Find the pearl. Save Tristan.

The pearl was somewhere in this mess, but how was I supposed to find it? I made my way to where I knew the fireplace would be on the other side of the room. My frustration grew with every step. I imagined Grandfather ordering his men to lock all of my parents' books away in the Solar so that he wouldn't see them every time he entered the library, and I didn't know whether to feel pity or fury.

Flotsam let out a small whimper, and I froze. Was Rodden coming, or worse, Emil? I strained, listening for the sound of footsteps. Instead, a different, much stranger sound reached my ears.

Music.

It was as if somewhere, miles and miles away, someone was singing a beautiful, lilting melody.

Maybe even a familiar melody—I couldn't quite hear enough to truly grasp it. Where was it coming from?

Calmer now, I moved through the stacks with purpose. I saw the fireplace and examined the mantle, but all I found was a thick layer of dust. No, it was coming from my right…an old, battered trunk tucked into the corner, all but obscured by shadows.

I hurried over and dropped to my knees. The lock was huge, shiny and silver, not a speck of rust. Holding my breath, I gave it a tug.

The lock snapped open, and a breathy laugh escaped me.

I lifted the lid and peered inside. For a moment, all I saw was darkness.

But there, in the bottom corner, was a shiny silver oyster shell. I lifted it carefully, hardly daring to breathe, and gently pried the shell open.

"Oh my goodness," I whispered.

The pearl was even more spectacular than it had been in Hydra's bubble. It wasn't just that it shone— it *glowed,* as if it held some light at its center that could never, ever be extinguished. I plucked it out, and the moment my fingertips grazed the surface, I heard that beautiful melody as if it were coming from inside me.

I let the oyster shell fall back into the trunk and held the pearl in my cupped palms. For the first time since my disastrous birthday party, I felt completely at peace. I knew it would be mad to say so out loud, but it felt as though this pearl had been waiting for me to find it. Like we belonged together.

With a contented sigh, I tucked the pearl safely into the pocket of my nightgown. I let out a soft whistle for the pups—Flotsam had been sniffing around a wardrobe, and I was fairly certain Jetsam had just relieved himself in the empty fireplace—and together, we headed to the Solar's double doors.

I stood there for nearly a minute, ear pressed to the wood, straining for any sounds of life. At last, I pulled the metal rod out from the handles and opened the doors.

Questions zipped through my mind as I crept down the corridor flanked by my pups. What now? Was I expected to simply walk into the ocean? How could I possibly survive a deep-sea search? How would I actually find Tristan? But even as I thought this, I felt no fear or worry. Because I had the pearl, and now I could take on any problem that came my way.

Hydra had led me to the pearl with her map. Maybe she could lead me to Tristan, too! Smiling, I picked up the pace as I made my way back to the secret passage. I'd nearly reached it when a shout from down the hall startled me.

"There she is!"

My head snapped up, and I saw Rodden sprinting toward me. Behind him—my stomach sank in

97

recognition—was Emil.

I threw myself into the passage and ran as fast as I could. The cold water dripping from the ceiling sent a pleasant shiver down my back. Flotsam and Jetsam kept pace on either side of me, a trio flying into the pitch blackness.

It was nearly a full minute before I heard the hum. *Heard* wasn't quite the right word, though. More like *felt*. Frowning, I slowed my pace slightly and grazed my hand along the damp wall. A slight vibration caused my fingertips to tingle, and it was growing stronger by the second.

Behind me, Flotsam and Jetsam suddenly stood stock-still, ears perked up, tails straight out. It was the same stance they took when they heard a fox rustling around the woods out behind the castle. I took a step back, squinting into the darkness ahead. The tide was low tonight, I knew that for certain. The ocean had rushed in and swept Tristan off, but that had been my fault. My tantrum.

Hadn't it?

Behind me, footsteps pounded—but quickly slowed to a halt.

"What is this witchcraft?" I heard Emil snarl.

A soft glow drew my attention to my feet. A pool of white light spilled around me, expanding to include Flotsam and Jetsam. I blinked, then pulled the pearl out of my pocket and gasped. It glowed bright as the moon in my palm, extending its magic—because it *was* magical, it had to be—like an orb around the three of us.

So, when the vibration turned to a low rumble, and that turned to a roar, I didn't feel a lick of fear. Unlike Emil and Rodden, who screamed and fled the passage.

Instead, I merely smiled, bracing myself as the ocean rushed in to take me away.

10

OCEAN UNIVERSE

The sea was so powerful, yet so gentle.

I had imagined Tristan caught up in a violent current that thrashed him against the walls of the passage as it whisked him out to the ocean. But I should have known that the sea would be kinder than that. It scooped me up, along with Flotsam and Jetsam, holding onto us securely as it rushed back out, and I felt as safe as I did in my own bed.

We whisked through the darkness, and after a few seconds, my lungs began to burn from holding my breath. I felt the pearl warming my palm and remembered my dream, when Hydra had filled my room with the ocean, yet I could still breathe.

But it hadn't been a dream, I reminded myself. It had been *magic*. Maybe I had to trust in that magic now.

I drew in a deep breath, then laughed, bubbles streaming from my mouth. *Thank you, Hydra!* I thought, and once again, I could have sworn I saw her smile flash in the dark.

Flotsam and Jetsam paddled along at my side, even though there was no need to paddle, and no point, either—the current would clearly take us wherever it wanted. I saw a fork up ahead; the passage moved up to the right, and down to the left. Up to the beach, no doubt, I thought. Tristan had said as much.

The current took us down.

It was stronger now, a suction feeling, as if we were spinning down the drain in a bathtub. I spotted a dark blue dot in the distant black growing larger by the second, and then...*whoosh!*

We burst into the ocean, twirling and spinning underwater. On instinct, I tried to kick my legs, but they felt strange and fluid beneath my nightgown. The water was much warmer here, and I laughed with delight as I spun around and around. I spotted Flotsam and Jetsam, tongues lolling as they batted at the streams of bubbles that followed us out of the crevasse in the rocks. Then I did a double-take.

Their black fur seemed darker, slick and shiny,

and their big brown eyes glowed greenish yellow. Their pointy ears were the same, and they still smiled those doggie smiles…but they almost seemed to be part-eel.

Was this part of the pearl's magic? I looked down at the gem in my palm, then gasped.

Eight tentacles, a shimmery blue, purple and green ombre like my birthday dress and utterly beautiful, flowed out in a perfect spiral around me. For a moment, I thought I was somehow sitting on top of an octopus, and I wiggled my legs to swim away—but the tentacles wiggled back, and it hit me.

They were *mine.*

Clutching the pearl to my chest, I wiggled my tentacles again. Then I kicked, and the power of eight limbs instead of two sent me rocketing up through the water. I laughed in awe, twisting and waving my tentacles, enjoying how graceful they were, yet so powerful. On land, I was constantly tripping over my own two feet. But now I felt like the most elegant dancer in the world.

Flotsam and Jetsam clearly felt the same. They flew around me like overly excited swans, swooping and diving and letting out little yips that sent more bubbles streaming through the water.

At last, the three of us slowed down, and I gathered my pups—my eel-pups—up in a hug. We gazed at our surroundings as the bubbles finally began to dissipate. Not far below us, the rocky floor sloped gradually down to a sharp drop-off into deeper blue waters. And beyond that…well, beyond that was the entire ocean.

And it was all mine to explore.

This was the grand adventure I'd always dreamed of. Minus the part where my cousin was the hostage of some…I frowned, my good mood bursting just like those tiny bubbles. Some evildoer, I supposed. I still had no idea who could have wanted my parents dead. The only enemies of the Kronbergs had been the Dark Ones. But Grandfather and Poseidon had defeated them long ago.

But whoever was behind all of this, I knew why they had Tristan. Why else were the children of royalty kidnapped? Ransom, of course. That had to be it.

In my mind, those masked pirates laughed and chugged rum and taunted Tristan, who was locked up in their brig. I flexed my fingers and grimaced. They would regret what they'd done. I'd make sure of that.

As Flotsam and Jetsam soared ahead of me, I pulled the shell compact from my pocket and opened it. I stared hard at the mirror, willing my reflection to waver and vanish, replaced by another vision of Tristan. But all I saw was my own violet eyes staring back at me. Sighing, I snapped the compact closed and held it tight as I swam after my pups.

Despite my determination to rescue my cousin, I found myself losing track of time as Flotsam and Jetsam and I explored. Deep beneath the surface, it was hard to tell whether the sun had begun to rise yet, and though I knew it must be at least close to morning, I felt as if I was in some ethereal, eternal night beneath the waves. As if time didn't even exist in the sea.

Besides, it wasn't important that I venture out far. I would have a far better chance at finding Tristan if I was thorough in my explorations of this area. After all, he had been kidnapped not even a full day ago. The sunken ship that was his prison couldn't be that far from the coast where the castle sat.

And, actually, searching for a ship was much harder than I'd imagined. I had always pictured the bottom of the ocean as a more or less flat surface, but now I saw it was as diverse a landscape as the ground above—if anything, even more so. There were hills and valleys, cliffs and mountains, reefs and trenches, all in vivid blues and greens and purples. The bright pink coral was more stunning than any treasure I'd ever seen, and the seaweed came in all shades of green. I thought of the sad gray stones that made up the castle, the austere portraits in dark tones covered with layers of dust, and wondered how I could ever return to living there after experiencing this vivid, beautiful world.

And oh, the creatures! I laughed as Flotsam chased a bright orange spider crab, which scuttled away sideways beneath a rock. The fish were like jewels in all shapes, sizes, and colors, all shimmering like coins as they darted out of our way. I spotted a few squid spinning slowly, their tentacles twirling so gracefully that I came to a stop for a few minutes to watch the performance. A dark green turtle zipped by, its speed startling me—they might have taken their time on land, but in the water they could really move!

There were jellyfish, too, nearly transparent and faintly glowing like billowing clouds. And there were creatures I had no name for: spindly ones, wormy ones, toothy ones, even winged ones! Some were fast while others crawled, some had no eyes while others seemed to lack a mouth. A few times, I inspected what I was certain was a rock or a plant, but when I got too close, it would scurry off, making me laugh with wonder.

Had Tristan been able to experience this? He would have loved it, science nerd that he was. I felt a pang in my chest at the thought of what he would say if he were here with me now, as we explored the sea together.

I was inspecting a yellow snail making its way across the sand when a distant sound reached my ears, causing the back of my neck to prickle. My hand went instinctively to the pearl in my pocket, because it almost sounded like that same melody. But then I realized this music was coming from much farther away.

"Do you hear it too, boy?" I whispered as Flotsam paddled over to my side. His ears were perked up, his yellow eyes alert. A moment later, Jetsam joined us, and we stared around in search of the source.

Then, in the distance, I spotted a shape in the dark blue water. Judging by how far away it was, I knew it must have been monstrously huge...the size of a ship. But no ship sailed *beneath* the waves. And as my eyes adjusted, I realized there were actually two shapes. No, three. Four...five.

I gasped, clapping my hand over my mouth as I realized what I was seeing. Mother and Father had told me about spotting them occasionally when they went out sailing, but I had never seen one for myself.

A whale.

A whole pod of whales. Mother would have been beside herself, I thought with a pang. The majestic creatures move with such grace, they brought tears to my eyes. I pulled Flotsam and Jetsam closer, and we stayed perfectly still, watching until the whales were out of sight.

"Well, that was something, wasn't it?" I asked, releasing my eel-pups. "Oh, I wish Tristan was here to see them!"

"*Violet?*"

I froze, hardly daring to believe my ears. That sounded like...but no. It was impossible. Wishful thinking.

"*Violet? Can you hear me?*"

The voice was tinny and small—but not distant. It was nearby.

It was coming from the compact!

"Tristan?" I fumbled with the shell, nearly dropping it in my haste to open it. "Tristan, is that you?"

I pried the shell open and let out a shout of triumph. Tristan beamed at me, his green eyes sparkling, his face perfectly framed by the mirror.

"I knew it! I knew you'd hear me!" He blinked, his expression turning confused. "Violet, where are you?"

"I'm in the ocean!" My voice trembled with emotion. Tristan really was alive. I was *talking* to him. "I'm coming to save you, Tristan! Where are you?"

"You're in the...what?!" Tristan gaped at me, and

I couldn't help but laugh.

"It's a long story! We all thought…Tristan, I thought you were…" My smile faded, and I swallowed hard as I settled down on a large, flat rock. "We thought you were dead. Drowned. What happened in the secret passage?"

Tristan sighed. "Honestly, I'm not sure. I was waiting for you when suddenly the tunnel began to… well, it felt like the walls were vibrating."

I nodded, listening intently. I remembered feeling the same vibration before the water had rushed into the tunnel. Only I'd had the pearl. How had Tristan survived?

"Then I heard a voice," Tristan went on slowly, his brow furrowed. "A woman's voice. I couldn't understand the words—it almost sounded like she was speaking a foreign language. And all of a sudden, I felt so drowsy, I could barely keep my eyes open. The last thing I remember was falling asleep in my wheelchair."

"And you woke up on the ship?" I asked, holding the compact closer.

Tristan looked confused. "Ship?"

"Yes!" Hastily, I told Tristan about Hydra visiting and showing me the image of him in a cage, and a sunken ship.

His eyes were as round as coins when I finished.

"Am I really on a sunken ship? But how is that possible? There's air, I can breathe…" He glanced about at his surroundings. "Although, I suppose it's not uncommon for pockets of air to exist in the ocean. Maybe I'm in the ship's brig, and there's an air pocket here due to the angle of the ship when it sunk. It's like that physics experiment I did once, turning a cup upside-down and submerging it in—"

"Enough with the science nerd talk," I said with a giggle. "Tristan, do you have any clue where the ship might be?"

He bit his lip. "No. I just woke up in this cage. I can't even really see much of the rest of the room— there's not much light in here. The only thing I can really see is a desk. I can barely reach it if I stick my arm through the bars. I checked the drawers, but they were all empty except for this compact mirror." He grinned at me. "I was going to see if I could take it apart, maybe use a shard of glass as a knife that could saw through the bars or something. But when I opened it, I saw *you*!"

I smiled back, although my mind was reeling. "Hydra gave me this compact," I told him. "She must have known you would have the other one. She led me to the pearl, too. She's been so helpful."

Tristan frowned slightly. "If she's so helpful, why doesn't she just tell you where to find me?"

I didn't respond right away. The truth was, I had wondered that myself. But when I thought of Hydra's voice in my head, encouraging me to summon Sprites at the party…and the way she'd filled my room with water, briefly letting me think I'd been about to drown…

"I think she's trying to teach me," I said at last.

"Teach you what?"

How to use my powers. Would it sound ridiculous if I said it out loud? I took a deep breath, but before I could say anything, Flotsam and Jetsam swam up and clung to my sides, whimpering loudly.

"What is it?" I asked, scratching the top of Flotsam's head. "Did you see a scary fish?"

"Violet?" Tristan's voice was suddenly distant. To my horror, I saw his image fading.

"Tristan!" I yelled, shaking the compact in frustration. But he was gone, and my reflection was back. I stared hard at the mirror, willing my cousin to return. Flotsam and Jetsam went perfectly still and silent, and suddenly, I realized why.

In the mirror, directly behind me, a giant mouth was opening wide, baring enormous, razor-sharp teeth.

11

SHARK WATERS

With a shriek, I spun around and swam backwards, clutching Flotsam and Jetsam tightly. A pair of beady, black eyes gleamed at me, though I was having a hard time focusing on anything other than those knife-like teeth.

The teeth of a shark.

"Hullo," the creature said.

I blinked. His voice was surprisingly high, and almost shy. I tore my gaze away from the teeth and realized two things.

First, the shark was trapped in a net. I could now see the thin black strands of a fisherman's net tangled around his fins. He must have been on the other side of the flat rock I'd been sitting on, and then he'd risen up a few feet off the sandy floor.

Second, he was only a baby.

I relaxed, but only a little. Baby or not, those teeth could still do some serious damage. And I didn't like the way he was eyeing Flotsam and Jetsam, like they might make a tasty snack.

"Hello," I replied at last, and the shark's grin widened. It was scary, but also sort of cute. "What's your name?"

"I'm Mac," he replied instantly. "My mum named me Mac after my great-uncle. He was the biggest great white shark in the whole ocean! I'm...well, I'm not done growing, but I don't think I'm gonna be that big." Mac eyed me sheepishly. "Sorry, I'm rambling. My cousins are always giving me a hard time about it."

"Nice to meet you, Mac," I said. "I'm Violet, and these are my dogs, Flotsam and Jetsam."

"Nice to meet you, too," Mac said. "Do you think you could help me out of this net? My mum will be wondering where I am. My cousins, not so much. We were actually playing a game of tag right before dinner when I got caught. Since I missed dinner, I bet they're worried...sorry, I'm rambling again. Um, so could you help me?"

At the mention of dinner, Flotsam let out a high-pitched whimper. I felt a little frightened too, but already, an idea was forming in my mind.

I lifted my chin and met Mac's gaze.

"I'll help you on two conditions."

"Anything!" the shark said eagerly. His tail wiggled a little, the same way Jetsam's did when he knew he was about to get a treat.

I narrowed my eyes. "One: my dogs are not dinner. Or breakfast or lunch or even a snack. They're completely and totally off-limits."

"Dogs?" Mac squinted. "Those look like eels to me. My mum taught me all about eels. She knows everything about the ocean. Some are electric and some are spiny, and the ones that live way down deep in the dark even *glow*—"

"Well, these are my dogs, Flotsam and Jetsam," I interrupted. "They might look like eels, but it's only temporary. The point is, you have to promise not to eat them. Got it?"

Mac looked slightly disappointed, but he nodded. "Got it."

"And two…" I paused, thinking carefully. "You have to help me find something. Or rather, someone."

Now, Mac looked nervous. "It's not a sea lion, is it? Not that I'm afraid of sea lions!" he yelped suddenly, glancing around. His voice had risen in volume and decibel, and I swam back a few feet. "I'm not afraid of sea lions or anything else! I'm a great white shark! Sea lions fear *me*!"

113

"Uh, no, it's not a sea lion," I said loudly, and Mac stared at me. "It's...it's a boy."

"A human boy?" Mac's voice returned to normal. "Humans can't live under the water. They live on land. My mum taught me that, too. Sometimes they sail on the ocean on boats, and sometimes they even swim in it, but they definitely don't stay for very long."

"I'm a human," I pointed out.

"Then why do you have those?" Mac attempted to gesture at my tentacles with his fin, then winced when the net pulled even tighter. I felt a wave of pity for him.

"Temporary, like I said," I went on, squeezing the compact tightly. "My cousin was kidnapped, and he's being held prisoner on a sunken ship. Do you know where that might be?"

Mac perked up. "I do! I do! I've seen a sunken ship! It's not far from here!"

"Really?" I exclaimed. "So, you can lead me there?"

"Yes!"

I glanced at Flotsam and Jetsam, who seemed slightly more relaxed. Mac gazed at us unblinkingly, waiting for me to respond with a hopeful smile.

"Okay, then," I said at last, swimming over to him. "But I'll warn you, Mac. I have powers. Seriously *strong,* seriously *dangerous* powers. And if you do anything to my pups, I swear I'll turn you into a—a snail!"

"I won't! I won't hurt them! I promise!"

So, I set to work untangling the net. It was caught on the bottom of the rock, as well, and it took several minutes of pulling and tugging to finally work the knots loose. With a joyful yelp, Mac sprang away from the rock and did a somersault.

Flotsam and Jetsam scurried behind me. "It's okay," I whispered, cuddling them close. "We can trust him."

Tentatively, Mac swam closer. Flotsam poked his head out from under my arm, then darted out and gave the shark a quick sniff. Mac giggled—an oddly high sound, but cute nonetheless—and I relaxed slightly.

"Okay," I said. "Take us to the sunken ship, Mac."

"This way!" Mac took off, and I pumped my tentacles and pushed off after him. Flotsam and Jetsam seemed comfortable now, but I couldn't help wondering if I'd made a mistake. Could we really trust a shark? All humans feared sharks, and for good reason.

But Mac was only a baby. And he really did seem to want to help.

Besides, he couldn't help being a carnivore. I didn't want to judge him based on his sharp teeth and black eyes the way people judged me for my silver streak and purple eyes. Just because a creature looked frightening didn't mean it *was* frightening. Maybe Mac would grow up to be a monster if everyone treated him like that's all he was.

I vowed right then and there that I wouldn't make that mistake.

The water grew cooler as Mac took us deeper and deeper, the water gradually turning from bright turquoise to more of a navy blue. At last, a familiar structure came into view. A ship, small but sturdy— or rather, it had been once.

I slowed to a halt, something tightening in my chest. I'd seen this ship before. And not just in Hydra's bubble. But it was so covered in barnacles and seaweed, the cabin partially crushed, the hull riddled with holes, that I couldn't quite place it. Then my eyes rested on the name painted along the side, peeling away and barely visible through a thin layer of moss: *SS Lydian*.

My mother's name.

This was my parents' ship. The ship they were on when they...when they were...

A choked sob escaped me, and for a moment, I fought the urge to swim away. I couldn't bear to look at the place where my parents had died, much less go inside. What if they were still in there? What if I saw their bones?

Was Tristan really trapped inside with their

bodies? Who would do such a terrible thing? Slowly, anger began to overtake my fear.

"Stay out here," I ordered Mac. "Keep an eye out for…well, anyone suspicious."

Mac nodded solemnly, then began to circle the *SS Lydian*. Turning, I steeled myself. Near the bottom of the hull was a hole large enough for me to swim through. The jagged planks of wood reminded me of Mac's teeth, and as I carefully made my way inside, I tried not to imagine that I was swimming straight into the mouth of a monster.

Inside, the water was a dark, murky green and filled with shadows. I moved cautiously, grateful for the comforting feel of Flotsam and Jetsam pressed up to my sides. Movement caught my eye, and I gasped as a spindly-legged creature scuttled back into the darkness before I could fully make it out. This ship had become a habitat, I realized, noticing a pair of eyes watching me from beneath an overturned chair. I probably should have been creeped out, but honestly, I liked the idea of sea creatures making themselves at home in my parents' ship. There was still life on board.

I made my way to the brig at the very back of the boat, straining for any sounds of movement. It was darker back here, since the brig had no portholes—that way, there was no chance for prisoners to escape.

"Tristan?" My voice was barely above a whisper.

"Are you here?"

I spotted the rusted bars of the cage and darted forward, nervously. But I knew well before I reached it that it was empty. The door of the cage was half off its hinges, the metal covered in blood-red rust. Besides, the entire boat was submerged. Wherever Tristan was, he had air. He could breathe.

This wasn't the cage I'd seen in Hydra's bubble. Tristan had never been here.

Bitter disappointment burned in my throat. I rubbed at my eyes, telling myself to get it together. This would have been too easy, after all. But I didn't care how long I had to search. I was going to find my cousin.

I swam up the spiral staircase that led from the brig to the cabin. I knew Tristan wouldn't be there, but I'd come this far—I couldn't leave this ship without a thorough search. Besides, I had to see if…well, I had to see what else might be here. No matter how sad or scary it might be.

I paused outside the door to the main suite of the cabin, resting my hands on the rotting wood. Jetsam gave my elbow an encouraging lick, and I braced myself.

Then I pushed the door open.

The suite was a wreck, but a quick glance around told me there were no bodies, no bones. Shoulders slumping in relief, I made my way inside. Fishing equipment, coats and hats, plates and cutlery littered the floor, all rusted or torn or broken. *These belonged to my parents,* I thought, picking up a fork with one prong missing. *Mother. Father.*

I squeezed the fork, then let it drift back down to the floor. Now that my relief had faded, more unsettling thoughts were bubbling up in my mind. My parents had been on a mission to speak to Poseidon, very much against Grandfather's will. Mother had been fiercely determined.

My Violet is barely nine years old. To tie her fate into this curse is nothing short of cruel. She must be allowed to choose her own path, to make her own choices. To do anything less would make us no better than the Dark Ones themselves.

My throat tightened as I recalled her words. I could so clearly picture my parents in this very suite, sailing farther out despite the storm brewing on the horizon, for *me.* But their ship had capsized before they could find Poseidon, and they had drowned.

So then *why* were my parents' bodies not here? I caught a glimpse of Mac through the porthole, still swimming dutifully in circles, and shuddered. Had the sharks found my parents? Had they ended up being a bloody feast for Mac's family? Maybe that was how he knew where this ship was…

Jetsam dug at a loose plank, letting out a whine. A glint of metal on the floor caught my eye, a merciful distraction from the gruesome images forming in my mind. I swam over and crouched down next to my pups, examining the planks. They were all rotting and molded, but one jutted up slightly higher than the rest, revealing a dark space beneath—a hiding spot. I pried the slippery, soft plank loose and stared down at the metal lockbox.

My parents had hidden this beneath the floorboards. But why? What was inside that was so important?

Head buzzing, I reached for the box and tugged at the lock. But it was made of gold, and it hadn't rusted a bit. I shook the lockbox, and it rattled.

Now my heart was pounding. I had to know what was inside, I *had* to. But how could I break this lock?

My gaze traveled to the porthole again, and I grinned.

"Mac? *Mac!*"

I slipped through the porthole, the lockbox tight in my hands. Flotsam and Jetsam tumbled out after me, and together we sped toward the baby shark.

"That's not a boy," Mac said, eyeing my hands. "That's a box. My mum taught me about boxes. Humans use them to keep—"

"Yes, I know." I tried not to sound too impatient. "My cousin wasn't in there after all. But I found this, and it—well, it's important. Can you open it for me?"

"Sure!"

I held out the lockbox, then let go. As it drifted to

the sand, Mac lunged forward and—

SNAP!

I gasped, propelling myself backward. Baby or not, those jaws were terrifyingly powerful. The box landed on the sand, and I saw the gold lock hanging off the hinge.

"Thank you!" I exclaimed, reaching for the box. Flotsam, Jetsam, and Mac gathered around to watch as I carefully lifted the lid.

An opal necklace lay inside, the iridescent blue-green gem shimmering as if it contained the entire sea. My eyes burned with sudden tears as memories of my mother flooded back, stronger than ever. How could I have forgotten this necklace? She'd always worn it—in fact, I couldn't think of a time I'd seen her without it around her neck. She'd even worn it to bed, tucked safely beneath her nightgown.

And yet...

I lifted the necklace from the box, gazing at the opal. And yet as the storm had raged and she'd been moments from death, she had taken the necklace off, locked it up in a box, and hidden it beneath the floorboards. Why?

Once again, my mind wandered back to pirates. I could picture my mother stowing this precious necklace away as the masked men boarded the ship...

No. I frowned, shaking my head. That didn't make any sense. Pirates never ventured this close to Elsinore, and anyway, why would Mother worry about hiding this one necklace when she knew she'd be fighting for her life?

Who had really killed my parents? And why didn't my mother want them to have this necklace? A new and even more terrible thought dawned on me.

My parents had been looking for Poseidon. What if they *had* found him? What if he reacted to mother's request the same way Grandfather had?

What if *Poseidon* had caused the storm that killed my parents?

My heart pounded wildly as I remembered Hydra's words. *The same evil that took your parents.* But Poseidon wasn't evil. He and Grandfather had worked together to banish the Dark Ones.

I know what you're hiding. About that girl. About the curse. Because of your foolish deal, Lydian was…

Lydian was killed. That was what Emil had been about to say, I was sure of it. I loathed Emil, but now I couldn't help thinking about what I'd overheard in the library secret passage in a new light. *Ever since the war against the Dark Ones, the pact with Poseidon, the king has been keeping a grave secret from all of us. One that puts Elsinore at risk more and more every day.*

I struggled to make sense of it. Emil had learned Grandfather was keeping a secret about the pact with Poseidon. Perhaps Grandfather knew Poseidon was actually evil? But then why wouldn't he take action? Especially after Poseidon had drowned his daughter and son-in-law. Was he simply too weak? Was that why Emil and the other council members thought he was putting Elsinore at risk?

As these thoughts flooded my mind, I slipped the necklace on. My throat felt tight as I imagined mother helping me with the clasp, and my fingers trembled.

"*Look out!*"

Startled, I looked up as Mac took off in a stream of bubbles. He dove for the hole in the hull, wriggling and squirming until he was inside. A moment later, I saw the two pinpricks of his eyes as he peered out from the darkness.

"Mac? Why are you…oh."

I swallowed hard. A group of sea lions had surrounded us while I'd been gazing at the necklace. They were almost Mac-sized, but eleven times scarier, with narrowed eyes and whiskered scowls that reminded me eerily of Grandfather's soldiers.

Not a group, I heard Tristan chiding as clearly as if he'd been standing right there. *A group of sea lions is called a* pod. *Or a colony, if they're in their natural habitat. But that right there? That's a pod.*

"You have been summoned, Violet Kronborg," the largest sea lion barked.

I lifted my chin and tried to keep my voice from wavering. "By whom?"

123

The sea lion's eyes glinted, but I couldn't tell if it was with malice or amusement.

"By one who does not take no for an answer."

Flotsam and Jetsam squeezed in at my sides, and I took a deep breath. What choice did I have?

"Okay. Lead the way."

Satisfied, the largest sea lion turned and swam off. I followed with my pups, the rest of the pod still surrounding us, swimming in perfect synchronization. I cast one last glance at the *SS Lydian* before it vanished from view, but there was no sign of Mac anywhere.

We ventured deeper still, the water growing uncomfortably chilly. Now that the shock had worn off, panic was starting to set in. Who was I about to meet? And what about Tristan? I berated myself for getting so distracted by the opal necklace. I'd allowed myself to get caught, and now I may never find my cousin.

At last, we reached the edge of an expanse of black sand. No, not sand.

My heart began to pound wildly when I realized what I was looking at. The sea lions had led me to the edge of a cliff, and below was a yawning black abyss, like the night sky without the benefit of the moon and the stars.

How deep did it go? I couldn't fathom. Nervously, I glanced at the largest sea lion, the one who seemed to be in charge. He stood stoically at the edge of the cliff, gazing out at the darkness. He seemed to be waiting for something. Then—*whoosh!*

I screamed as a swarm of the strangest and most terrifying sea creatures I'd ever seen soared over the top of the cliff. Spiky, eyeless squids thrumming with an odd purple light zipped around me and my pups, long strands of seaweed clenched in their shockingly huge jaws. Before I could react, they'd wrapped me up like a mummy. I barely caught a glimpse of Flotsam and Jetsam struggling in their own seaweed wraps before there was a great tug, and then the awful creatures dragged us over the edge and straight down into the abyss.

Now I couldn't even scream. I was past terror, past any sort of rational thought. We plummeted down at breakneck speed, but I didn't struggle against my bonds, because the idea of breaking loose, of floating alone in this darkness, was somehow even more petrifying then being dragged down by glowing, razor-toothed squid.

At last, we began to slow, although my pulse kept up a rapid rat-a-tat-tat in my ears. Little pinpricks of light flickered here and there in the black, slowly growing brighter, like incoming stars.

No, not stars. They were sea creatures. Jellyfish, tube worms, viperfish, spider crabs—only they glowed, like the squid. The closer they drew, the more they illuminated my surroundings. I could see rocks below, the shadows of even more creatures slithering and squirming and crawling.

For a moment, I forgot to be afraid. I thought I'd understood how vast and incredible the ocean was, but clearly I had no idea.

It wasn't just another world. It was another *universe.*

The water was truly frigid now, and I wondered if my skin was turning blue. I wiggled against my seaweed bonds and managed to work my hand into my pocket. My fingers grasped the pearl, and it began to glow, surrounding me, Flotsam, and Jetsam with a dim but beautiful light. A wave of wonderful warmth rushed through me, and I sighed with relief.

At last, we landed on the rocks. I braced myself as several of the squid lunged at me, jaws snapping— but then the seaweed fell away, and they swam off, disappearing into the inky blackness.

"Well, that was something," I said to Flotsam and Jetsam. They stared up at me dolefully, and I wondered if they regretted following me into the west wing.

I turned slowly and saw the mouth of a cave. Or at least, I thought it was a cave at first. But the closer we moved, the more it began to resemble the skeleton of some unfathomably enormous creature with a gaping maw.

A soft green light emanated from inside. Whoever had summoned me was waiting. I kept my hand tight around the pearl as I stepped inside, Flotsam and Jetsam right behind me. My fingers grazed the compact, but now was not the time to contact Tristan. If I was about to meet whoever had kidnapped him, they wouldn't be happy to know Tristan and I had found a way to communicate.

Inside, I found myself in a long corridor lined with pointy rocks. Or teeth, I told myself, and I tried not to look at them very hard. But it was hard to ignore the feeling that I was stepping straight into the mouth of a monster.

At last, the corridor widened into a large hall. In the center was a giant cauldron, and from the ceiling, dark pink plants dangled lifelessly. But my eyes went straight to the tall figure at the very back of the hall. My mouth fell open as our eyes locked.

"Hello, my dear," said Hydra.

12

OPAL

"H-Hydra?" I stammered, unable to believe my eyes.

She looked exactly as she had in my dream—or vision, or whatever that had been. Only now, the odd light of the cave gave her skin a greenish sheen, and her incisor teeth were just a tiny bit larger and sharper than what I remembered.

A wave of relief shuddered through me, and I moved closer.

"I'm so glad to see you! Thank you so much for the map—I found the pearl, see?"

I held the glowing pearl up, and Hydra nodded, her expression pleased.

"Well done, my dear. I summoned you to find out how your rescue mission has gone so far?"

My spirits fell as I remembered Tristan. "I've searched and searched, but the ocean is so…well, it's so *big*," I said helplessly, feeling foolish. "I know he's on a sunken ship, but I have no idea how to find it, I even asked a shark for help, and he brought me to a ship, but it wasn't…Tristan wasn't there. It was my parents' ship, though, and I went inside and found…"

I trailed off, because Hydra had gone very still. Her eyes flashed, and something about her expression made me swallow the last few words. *My mother's opal necklace.*

"You found what, exactly?" she asked, her voice a touch too sweet, like honey gone bad.

I could feel the opal pressed against my chest, and I was grateful it was tucked under my top and covered with hair. I looked away from Hydra, pretending to study the rest of the hall.

"Some of my parents' things," I finished weakly. "Fishing equipment, forks and knives, things like that. I think maybe they were in the middle of a meal when…when whoever attacked them showed up."

Once again, I thought of Poseidon. I had never seen him before, but there were sketches in the history books Tristan loved of a massive man with broad shoulders and a long beard. He always looked fierce, hand gripping a trident, bushy brows narrowed over piercing eyes.

Evil. Could it really be true? Was Poseidon not a hero, but a villain?

If he was, and Grandfather had made a pact with him—a pact that involved me—why wouldn't Grandfather pull out of it? There were only two answers to that question. One was that Grandfather was too afraid to cross Poseidon.

The other was that Grandfather was evil, too.

A strange, cold feeling settled in the pit of my stomach. No, I couldn't allow myself to think that way. For all of his faults, Grandfather was a good and kind man and a benevolent king.

I did my best to force those thoughts from my mind. Hydra hadn't responded yet, and I still couldn't bring myself to meet her gaze. I focused instead on a patch of wall on the right. It might have been my imagination, but I almost thought it had an odd shimmer to it. As if it wasn't really a wall, but a mirage of a wall.

"I—I need your help, Hydra," I continued desperately. "I know you've already helped me so much more than anyone ever has, but I don't know how to find Tristan. Can you show him to me again? Maybe I can figure out where he is!"

"With pleasure," Hydra replied, and she immediately conjured her bubble.

My heart fluttered when I saw my cousin. He

looked alert, despite the bags under his eyes. In fact, he almost looked as if he was listening to something intently. I examined his cage, but saw nothing, no clue as to where I might find him.

"I can take you to him."

Hydra's words took a moment to register. I tore my gaze away from Tristan and blinked at her.

"What?"

"I can take you to your cousin," Hydra said softly. "In fact, nothing would delight me more. But I need a favor first."

My pulse quickened. "Yes! Anything!"

Hydra sighed. "The problem is, I'm trapped in this deep-sea trench, confined to the darkness. There is a curse upon me, and it prevents me from traveling to any part of the ocean the sunlight can reach."

"A curse?" The word felt odd on my tongue. "Who would put a curse on you?"

"A wicked, wicked person," Hydra said gravely. "But that's no concern of yours…at least, not at the moment. Now, the source of the curse's magic is three gems. Those gems have been scattered, hidden in various parts of the ocean. If you can find them and bring them to me, I can destroy them and break the curse. Then I will release Tristan."

I was so wrapped up in the idea of gems and curses that it took a full minute for her last sentence to properly register.

I will release Tristan.

"You," I whispered, stepped back. Hydra watched me, her expression impassive, almost imperious. "You took him."

I waited for her to deny it, but she remained silent. My head started to spin.

"You used your powers to flood the secret passage. *You're* holding Tristan prisoner—did you do this just so I'd help you find the gems?"

Hydra lifted a shoulder. "I needed insurance, my dear. Surely you can understand that."

"All that stuff you said about helping me with my powers…you didn't mean it, did you. You were just using me."

As my fury began to build, so did my power. I could feel it rushing up inside me, causing my skin to tingle with heat, and I welcomed it.

"I'll never help you," I spat. "I'll find Tristan on my own."

Hydra let out a heavy sigh. "You see, this is why I had to take him to begin with, my dear. I knew a Kronborg would never help me out unless I had something they held dear in my grasp."

And then she lifted her hands. There was a bright flash and a *whoosh,* and I heard Flotsam and Jetsam yelp in alarm. I screamed, reaching blindly for them, but it was too late.

"You see, my dear?" Hydra smiled. "Insurance."

I stared at my pups, both gazing helplessly at me from inside a bubble. I lunged for them, but the moment I touched the bubble, I flew backwards as if I'd been shoved by some invisible giant. Tears pricked the corners of my eyes as I stared at Flotsam and Jetsam. I was horrified to realize that their eel qualities were gone—they were just two innocent little pups in the very deepest part of the ocean, and Hydra's bubble was the only thing keeping them from drowning.

"Please…" I sobbed. "Please, please don't…"

"I won't pop the bubble," Hydra said. "I promise to keep them safe. So long as you fetch the gems like a good little girl."

"How am I supposed to find three gems that could be anywhere in the ocean?" I cried desperately. "Where would I even start looking?"

"Just follow your instincts, my dear," Hydra said with a smile. "It's in your blood."

With that, her eyes flashed bright green, and another wave of power rushed at me, sending me tumbling out of the cave. I shot up through the darkness and soared too high and too fast, like an out-of-control bird. Squeezing my eyes closed, I clutched at the pearl in my pocket, which instantly filled me with warmth and light.

At last, I began to slow, and I opened my eyes. Immediately, I regretted it.

The cave was out of sight. I was completely alone in the dark abyss. For a moment, the fear I felt was almost crippling. But I couldn't afford to panic. If I panicked, if I failed, then Tristan and Flotsam and Jetsam would pay the ultimate price.

Fear would do me no good. No, what I needed was *anger*. Because when I was angry, I could summon my powers.

When I was angry, I could do anything.

I forced myself to picture Tristan in his cage and my pups in that bubble, frightened and cold and lonely. Then I imagined Hydra laughing at me. I thought about the way she'd tricked me, setting up this whole trap so that I would break the curse and free her. And I'd fallen for it hook, line, and sinker.

Red-hot rage spread through me like burning fuel, and I opened my eyes. Then I pumped my tentacles and shot up through the darkness, making my way back to the part of the ocean touched by light.

I would find those gems and save my loved ones from Hydra. But if she thought I was going to let her get away with this, she was sorely mistaken.

13

AMETHYST

To my great surprise, Mac was waiting for me at the top of the cliff. He swam back a few feet in alarm when I burst over the edge.

"Violet! You're okay!" he said with a wide grin. "But wait…where are your pups?"

My throat tightened, and I struggled not to burst into tears. I didn't have time to cry. I had to act.

"They're being held captive," I told Mac, my voice cracking. "I was tricked by an awful sea witch."

Witch. The word startled me. After all, hadn't I been called a witch by practically every citizen in Elsinore? It was the worst insult I could think of. But as soon as I said it, I realized it wasn't just an insult.

Hydra really was a sea witch.

"That's horrible!" Mac exclaimed. "What does she want?"

I sank to the sand, suddenly exhausted, and told Mac the whole story about the gems and the curse.

"So, if I bring her all three gems, she promised to release them," I finished. "And I know I shouldn't. I mean, she's *evil*, Mac! Whoever put that curse on her was doing the whole ocean a favor. But I have to find the gems, even if it means setting Hydra free. I can't just let Tristan, Flotsam, and Jetsam die!"

A tear slipped down my cheek, and I wiped it away hastily.

"Do you trust her?"

I stared at Mac. "What? No, of course not! She tricked me!"

"Then why do you think she'll actually let your cousin and the pups go if you help her?"

I felt my mouth open and close. Then I buried my face in my hands. Mac was right, of course. Even if I somehow found the three gems and brought them back to Hydra, what in the world had ever made me believe she'd be true to her word?

There was a very real chance that Tristan, Flotsam, and Jetsam were doomed, no matter what I did.

Suddenly, Mac burst into noisy tears.

"I'm so sorry, this is all my fault," he blubbered. "My cousins are right. I'm the worst great white shark ever! I'm the shame of the family! I'm not fit for fins!"

I lowered my hands and stared at him in confusion. "What are you talking about?"

"The s-sea lions!" the baby shark wailed. "I'm terrified of them! I was lying when I said I wasn't! I should've fought them when they surrounded you! That's what my mum would've done, and all my cousins, too! They would've acted like *real* sharks. But I ran away like a coward!"

I felt a wave of sympathy for the blubbering shark. "Those sea lions were pretty intimidating," I told him gently. "They reminded me of Grandfather's soldiers."

"Yes, but you're a human," Mac said miserably. "I'm a *shark*. A great white shark! Great white sharks aren't supposed to be afraid of sea lions. We eat them! *They* fear *us*! At least, that's what my mum says. My cousins, too. They chase sea lions for fun, and they never invite me along because they know I'll spoil the whole thing. But I can't help it. The sea lions scare me. My family is always giving me a hard time about it." He sniffed loudly. "I'm a coward. I'm not a shark, I'm just a great big scaredy cat!"

He burst into tears once again, and I hurried over and put my arm over his fin. "There, there," I said comfortingly, wondering how I could have ever been afraid of this sad little baby shark. "It's okay, Mac.

Everyone feels scared sometimes. You'll find your courage."

"Will I?" Mac's beady black eye gazed at me dolefully. "I just hid behind the ship when the sea lions took you away. I let it happen. It's all my fault, like I said."

"No," I told him firmly. "This is Hydra's fault, and no one else's."

"You're so nice!" Mac wailed, sniffling again. "My mum always says humans aren't so nice. They only visit the ocean when they want to eat something that lives in it. But you're not like a regular human. Y-you really aren't mad at me?"

I watched as he blew his nose on a flatfish that had the misfortune of passing by at the wrong moment. It flew off in a huff, and for the first time since finding my parents' ship, I giggled.

"I'm not mad at all. I don't blame you, Mac. I promise."

Mac gave me a watery smile. "I'm going to make it up to you," he said suddenly. "I promise. I'll help you find the gems. And then…and then *we'll* be the ones with the insurance!"

I blinked. "What do you mean?"

"That's what Hydra said, right?" Mac asked. "She's keeping your pups as insurance to force you to find the gems."

"Right…"

"Well, once we have the gems, we'll keep them as insurance until she returns Flotsam and Jetsam!" Mac said. "And Tristan, too! We'll show that nasty sea witch she messed with the wrong octopus! Er, human!" Octosapien!

I giggled, pondering this, staring thoughtfully at the shark. "That's a good idea," I said finally. "Thanks, Mac."

He beamed at me, pointy teeth flashing, and I grinned back. I might have lost my pups, but at least I wasn't completely alone. A frightened baby shark was better than nothing, and besides, Mac was really sweet.

"Of course, I have no idea where to start looking," I said with a sigh. "I don't suppose you know anything about these gems?"

"Let's see," Mac mused. "My mum never told me any stories about curses or gems…"

Stories. I gasped, and Mac looked at me in alarm. "What?"

"Mac, you're a genius!" I cried. "Stories—when we were little, Tristan's mom used to tell him a story about a mystical amethyst."

"An ame-what?"

"Amethyst! It's a purple gem!"

"Oooh!" Mac said eagerly. "Do you remember the story? I love stories! My mum tells me stories all the time, mostly about my great uncle and how he swam around the whole world twice and also fought a blue whale and oh, there was one story about how he fought an honest-to-goodness *kraken* and…"

As Mac rambled on and on, I pulled out the compact and opened it. Tristan had told me that old tale about the amethyst so many times, but I'd never paid close attention. Well, except for the part about how the gem was the exact color of my eyes.

"Tristan? Tristan, can you hear me?" I whispered, gazing at the mirror. "Tristan, please, I—I need you…"

Mac fell silent, watching me sympathetically. And to my surprise and relief, the mirror seemed to flicker, and Tristan's face replaced mine.

"Violet!" He sounded scared. "Are you okay?"

"Yes! But listen, I need your help—"

"She's…trust her! I didn't…trick!"

"What?" I frowned, holding the compact closer. "Tristan, I can't hear you!"

He looked frantic now, and my heart skipped a beat. "…a trap! Don't do…says!"

"What trap? What are you talking about?" I cried, but already, my cousin was gone.

With a groan, I closed the compact and tried to think. What had Tristan and I been talking about before we'd been cut off last time? After a moment, I remembered. I had been about to tell him that I thought Hydra was trying to teach me to use my powers. Then Tristan's image had faded, and I had met Mac.

What had happened since then to make Tristan so frightened? Had he learned something about his captor? *Trust her…trick…a trap…don't…*

I let out a frustrated sigh. I needed to save Tristan and Flotsam and Jetsam—everything else could wait. Right now, I just had to focus on finding those gems so I could force Hydra to return my loved ones safely.

"The story about the amethyst," I said out loud, hoping to jog my more details from my memory. "It was supposed to be very powerful, my aunt said. But she never said what kind of power it had, just that it needed to be protected." I sat up straighter. "It had *protectors*. It was guarded by…by sea otters!"

"Sea otters?" Mac repeated excitedly.

"Yes!" I shot up, grinning widely. "Mac, do you know where we can find the sea otters?"

"I do!" Mac stared at me for a moment. Then he let out a joyful help, flipping in a circle. "I do! I do! I can help, I can help!"

I hugged the baby shark tightly. "Then lead the way!"

We set off together, and for the first time since Hydra's cave, I felt a thin ray of hope pierce through the darkness of my fear.

The sea otter habitat turned out to be just over an

hour's swim away, a little bit closer to the coast of Elsinore—but not so close that I was worried about anyone spotting me. Mac and I chatted the whole way, him telling me stories about his family, how brave his mum was and how his cousins teased him mercilessly; me telling him about Grandfather's overprotectiveness and the wall that would soon block my view of the ocean.

"That's terrible," Mac said, his eyes wide. "My family teases me sometimes, but they're never cruel. Although one of my cousins did leave a half-eaten seal behind my favorite hiding rock to scare me the other day."

I tried to laugh, but it came out forced and fake. "Grandfather isn't cruel. I mean, he doesn't mean to be."

Mac gave me a sympathetic smile and said nothing. But I knew what he was thinking. If keeping your own granddaughter prisoner wasn't cruel, then what was?

As we swam on in silence, the pact Grandfather had made with Poseidon continued nagging at me. I struggled to focus on the facts and not speculate. I didn't know that Poseidon had killed my parents. I *did* know that my parents had been on their way to see him when they died. Their deaths might have been an accident—Hydra had told me otherwise, but, clearly, I couldn't trust her. But then there was the opal necklace my mother had hidden under that loose plank...

My fingers wandered to the pendant, and I grimaced. Hydra might have lied about other things, but my gut told me she'd been telling the truth about that. My parents' death was no accident.

Everything I'd learned churned endlessly in my mind, and I couldn't make any sense of it. Especially when it came to *me*. How could I possibly fit into the pact Poseidon and Grandfather had made to defeat the Dark Ones? Emil had said something about a curse... but I hadn't even been born yet! I wrinkled my nose as I pictured the sniveling councilman. Whatever he thought about Grandfather, he was *wrong*. None of the rumors about the family curse or me being a witch had even started until after my parents had died. It had nothing to do with Grandfather and Poseidon. Emil was just taking advantage of peoples' fear to make the king seem weak.

And it was working. My stomach tightened at the thought. Emil already had a few council members on his side. As for the people of Elsinore, they'd all been witnesses to what I'd done at my birthday party.

For a moment, I thought I might be sick. If Emil really was about to stage a coup, he just might be successful.

Gritting my teeth, I swam faster. I had to worry about saving Tristan and my pups first. Then we'd figure out what to do about Emil.

The water gradually lightened to a bright turquoise, and the temperature was pleasantly warm. I thought of Hydra trapped in her cave in the darkest, coldest part of the ocean and, for a brief, strange moment, I felt a wave of sympathy for her. She was a prisoner too, after all. Although she must have done something to deserve her punishment. I definitely hadn't.

And that's when it hit me for the first time: Hydra and I were both cursed.

I began to slow my pace without realizing it, vaguely aware of Mac moving ahead of me. Hydra was cursed, trapped in the trench. And I was part of a curse, too, according to my mother's letter.

Could it be the *same* curse?

But the one my mother mentioned had to do with the war with the Dark Ones. Had Hydra been involved, somehow? It seemed unlikely. Even Tristan, who devoured history books like they were honey tarts, had never heard of Hydra.

"It's right over here!" Mac said in a loud whisper, pulling me from my thoughts. I put on a burst of speed to catch up to him. Together, we peered around a cliff, and I saw a thick forest of kelp spread out below us. I noticed movement, and once I realized what I was seeing, I let out a soft "*Oh!*"

The sea otter habitat was nestled in the kelp forest, a whole neighborhood of rows of caves with bright green seaweed doors and beautiful coral decorations. From here, I could see the sea otters bustling about, laughing and chatting. Some were bringing in armloads of shellfish, while others swept their caves or polished their coral. It was a very pleasant scene, and I couldn't help but smile as I thought about what Tristan would say if he could see it.

"Come on, let's go ask them about the amethyst!" I said, moving forward eagerly.

But Mac didn't move. "Right now? It looks like they're busy…"

His eyes didn't quite meet mine. He was afraid of the sea otters, too, I realized with a wave of sympathy.

I chewed my lip for a moment, wondering what to do. Then inspiration struck. "You know, Mac, I'm going to need a lookout! Why don't you stay here and keep an eye on things, okay?"

"Okay!" Mac said eagerly. Then his face fell. "But what if the sea lions find us again? I—I can't fight them, I just can't."

"It's okay. Just…" I looked around quickly, then snatched up a nearby conch shell. "Just blow into this to warn me!"

Mac brightened up as he too the conch shell. "You got it, Violet! I won't let you down!"

"I know you won't," I said with a smile. Then I swam around the side of the cliff and headed to the sea otter habitat alone.

14

OTTER WATERS

As I drew closer, I began to feel a little nervous myself. After all, if Tristan's story was right and the sea otters were guarding one of the gems that kept Hydra imprisoned, that meant I was the enemy. I was here to steal from them. But I couldn't let them know it.

"Hello, there!"

I gasped and spun around to find myself facing a sea otter. His round face was split into a big smile, baring surprisingly pointy teeth. "Oh! Hello!" I said, doing my best to sound calm.

"Can I help you? Are you lost?"

"I, um…" I paused, wishing I'd taken the time

to come up with an excuse for being here. Then I realized the otter had already provided me with one. "Yes, I'm lost! I'm not from this part of the ocean."

"I can see that!" the otter said with a little laugh. "I've never seen an octopus like you before. I'm Murray, by the way."

He held out his paw, and I noticed a little furry pocket under his arm that bulged slightly.

"I'm Violet," I said, shaking his paw.

"Well, Violet, I'm sure we can get you all straightened out," said Murray. "But first, are you hungry? Please say yes! We've been preparing a feast all day!"

"Oh, I'm not really…" I began, but then my stomach betrayed me with a loud rumble.

Murray laughed again, and I couldn't help but giggle, too. "Well, I guess I'm a little hungry," I admitted. The last time I'd eaten anything was my birthday party, which felt like a lifetime ago.

"Then you showed up just in time!" Murray gestured for me to follow him, and I did. He kept up a steady stream of chatter as we swam, but I was too busy taking in every detail of the habitat, looking for anything that might be a good hiding spot for a powerful gem. The problem was, there were hundreds of places the amethyst might be hidden. As we passed cave after cave, I could see hammocks and shelves lined with tools and little jars and bowls inside. Was the amethyst in one of those caves?

No, that didn't seem safe enough. Not for a cursed gem holding a sea witch captive. Something like that would require an extra-special, extra-safe hiding spot.

This was going to be harder than I'd thought.

We reached the largest cave at the end of the row, where dozens of sea otters were bustling around. As they chattered away and gestured excitedly, I noticed that they all had furry underarm pockets like Murray's, and each one bulged a little bit. It was odd-looking, but also kind of cute.

When we entered the cave, my eyes widened at the sight of a long table spread with a seafood buffet to rival any feast I'd ever had at Kronborg Castle. There were piles of bright red lobster, sunset orange crabs, blue-gray clams, and shiny black mussels. There were also plates of what looked like a seaweed salad, along with bouquets filled with water lilies. The centerpiece was a massive squid, tentacles curled artfully around the platter. I smiled when I imagined how Sirena would approve.

"Presentation is a key part of cooking that many chefs forget," she'd told me once. "When we eat, we do so with our eyes before our mouths take a single bite."

She was absolutely right. I was feasting with my eyes before Murray had even pulled out my chair.

"Friends, we have a guest for our feast today!" Murray announced, and I felt my cheeks flush as dozens of pairs of black eyes stared at me curiously. "This is Violet, and she's a little lost...and a *lot* hungry!"

The otters laughed, and I did too, feeling slightly more relaxed.

"Thank you so much, Murray," I said. "This looks delicious. I'm honored to be a guest here."

Chatter broke out again, and I helped myself to a crab. Then I frowned, picking up my plate and looking for a knife or fork. Was I supposed to break the crab open with my bare hands?

Glancing around, I watched as the sea otters all dug into the pouches beneath their arms and pulled out rocks. They set to work pounding open crabs, lobsters, clams, and mussels, and I smiled. So that little mystery was solved—they kept rocks in those arm pockets! But I still had no idea how I was going to eat.

"Not to worry, Violet, not to worry!" Murray said jovially. "You can share with me and Priscilla."

The otter on the other side of Murray gave me a wide smile and held out a flat gray rock. "Here you go!"

"Thank you," I said, accepting it and smashing my crab open. "These are really handy! I can see why you carry them around."

149

"Oh, they're handy for much more than opening crabs," Murray told me, taking the rock and cracking open a clam. "Rocks are the most useful tools in the ocean. When sea otters are just wee pups, we find one special rock—a rock we have a connection with. We keep it in our pockets at all times, and for the rest of our lives." He glanced at me, as I swallowed a bite of crab. "Do you have an object like that? Something so precious, you don't know what you'd do if you lost it?"

I started to say no, then remember my mother's opal necklace tucked away under my nightdress. She'd worn it all her life, like the sea otters carried their rocks.

"Yes, I do," I said softly, and Murray smiled.

He handed the rock back to Priscilla, who set to work opening up a lobster. I glanced at Murray curiously. Had he lost his lifetime rock? The thought made me sad...but then I remembered seeing that bulge beneath his arm. So, he did have a rock, he didn't want to use it on food. Maybe it was too special.

After finishing my crab, I moved on to a lobster. It was soft and buttery and sweet and for a while, I forgot about my mission and focused on eating as much as I could. After all, I had no idea when I'd have the chance to eat again, and I had to keep up my strength. I pictured Mac hovering around the cliff, nervously looking around for sea lions, and felt a bit guilty. Maybe I could smuggle him a few clams in my pocket. It was the least I could do.

Nearly an hour later, I sat back in my chair and patted my full belly. "That was amazing," I told Murray, and I meant it. "Thank you so much."

"Of course, of course!" Murray grinned his pointy-toothed grin. "But the feast isn't over yet. We always have a good story for dessert. Stories are good for digestion, aren't they?" he added, and the other otters laughed and nodded in agreement.

I laughed, too—and then suddenly, I realized this was my chance.

"I know a good story!"

"Do you now?" Murray's eyes glinted. "How about it, everyone? Shall we let our guest tell us a tale?"

"Yes, go on!"

"Hear, hear!"

I sat up straighter, trying to get my thoughts together. I had to be careful in how I worded this. I didn't want to make the otters suspicious of me.

Clearing my throat, I began.

"Once upon a time, there was a mystical amethyst."

The change in the atmosphere was immediate. Priscilla dropped her rock with a loud clatter. The otters' smiles vanished, and their eyes widened, then immediately narrowed. Gulping, I glanced at Murray, but his friendly grin was gone. When he spoke, his voice had lost its bubbly warmth.

"Go on."

Uncertainly, I continued. "This amethyst was said to have extraordinary power. The power to do wonderful, fantastical things..."

I paused, thinking. The cave was silent as a tomb as the sea otters waited for me to continue.

"The power to save those who need saving," I said finally. My throat tightened as I pictured Tristan, Flotsam, and Jetsam. "But the amethyst was lost in the ocean. Until—"

"That's not how the story goes."

I fell silent as Murray glowered at me. His voice had gone hard, and the look in his eyes sent a chill up my spine.

"You know this story, too?" I asked, doing my best to sound nonchalant.

"Everyone does," he said shortly. "The amethyst does indeed have extraordinary power—the power to keep a great evil at bay. The sea otters were entrusted with the task of keeping the amethyst safe, and this is not a task we take lightly. Where did you say you heard this tale?"

"M-my cousin told me," I stammered. "Well, his mother told him, so I guess it was my aunt who…I mean, I thought it was just a fairy tale. I didn't mean to offend anyone."

"Hmmph," Murray said.

"Maybe someone else should tell a story instead," I suggested. "It seems I'm not very good at it."

That caused a few otters to chuckle, and I relaxed slightly.

"I'll take a turn!" Priscilla said, fixing her gaze on me. She bared her teeth, but I couldn't tell if it was in a smile or a grimace. "My tale has the most wicked villain you could possibly imagine."

"Now, Priscilla," Murray said making a half-hearted attempt to shush her. But already, sea otters up and down the table were pounding their fists on the rock and cheering for the tale.

"Once upon a time, the world was bright and beautiful. All of the creatures on both land and sea lived in perfect harmony."

As Priscilla began her story, I exhaled and leaned back in my chair. But my relief didn't last long. I'd completely blown it—Murray definitely didn't trust me anymore, and as soon as this feast was over, he'd no doubt escort me right out of the habitat.

"Until one day, a dark power began to rise. An evil so unstoppable, it threatened to dominate both land and sea."

I was starting to feel desperate. The amethyst was somewhere nearby, and I had just ruined my chances of finding it! For a moment, I felt annoyed with Murray.

But then I reminded myself that he was right not to trust me. The amethyst *was* keeping a great evil at bay—Hydra. And I was planning on stealing it from the otters, just like she wanted me to. I was helping a sea witch, trying to trick a friendly otter clan who had sworn to protect one of the three gems that kept her prisoner.

I really was a villain.

"For many years, it seemed as though the enemy couldn't be stopped. It threatened the lives of sea otters and whales, starfish and sharks, birds and horses and even humans."

My eyes suddenly felt hot. I didn't want to be a villain. I didn't want to help Hydra. But what about Tristan, and Flotsam and Jetsam? Was I just supposed to abandon them to their fates? Mac had said that I could use the gems as insurance to force Hydra to free my loved ones—but what then? Would I really hand the gems over and turn her loose on the entire ocean and all the wonderful creatures that lived here? Or would I try to fight her?

And if I did fight her, was there any chance at all that I could win?

I thought about everything Hydra had done: the way she'd visited me in my dreams, filling my bedchamber with the ocean, sending that flood into the secret passage to kidnap Tristan. If she was that powerful while imprisoned and under a curse, I couldn't imagine what her powers were like when she was free. And me? All I'd managed to do was knock over some guards, break a few windows, and shake a few stones loose from the wall. That was nothing.

I wouldn't stand a chance.

I closed my eyes, struggling not to cry. *Focus on your anger,* I told myself, squeezing my hands into fists. *Fear makes you weak. Anger is power.*

The image of that massive creature rising out of the ocean in my dreams filled my mind, and my breathing slowed. I opened my eyes, feeling calmer, stronger, surer of myself.

I would find the amethyst, no matter what it took. I would find all of the gems. And once my loved ones were safe, I would defeat Hydra. I wasn't sure how, but I swore right then and there that I would find a way.

But first, I had to figure out where the sea otters had hidden the amethyst. And I had to do it fast.

Priscilla was still telling her story. But as I looked around the table, I realized with a horrible jolt that no one was watching her.

Every single pair of black, beady eyes was locked onto me.

"Finally, the king of the land and the king of the sea decided their only choice was to work together," Priscilla said slowly, staring at me unblinkingly.

Her words were like an electric shock, and I sat up straight.

She was talking about Poseidon and Grandfather!

"They made a pact. A curse," Priscilla drawled, sounding as though she was relishing every word. "The evil would be vanquished. But it takes a powerful magic to keep such evil at bay. It takes true unity. The kings promised a marriage of land and sea, a marriage that would seal the curse permanently."

My heart fluttered uncertainly. Marriage of land and sea? What did that mean?

"But the evil one was crafty," Priscilla said, and several sea otters murmured and nodded in agreement. The way they were all staring at me was making my skin crawl. "A master of manipulation. She knew that finding the gems before the marriage took place was her only chance of escaping the curse."

Gems? Suddenly, I wished I'd been paying closer attention to Priscilla's story. I stared at her, my throat dry as she lowered her voice. Her next words dropped heavily, like stones in a pond.

"So, she sent an octopus to find them. But the sea otters were too smart for her."

I had royally messed up by saying something about the amethyst.

"Fortunately, the sea otters defeated the octopus," Priscilla said quietly. "And they all lived happily ever after."

Silence hung over the table. I knew, with sudden and absolute certainty, that the sea otters were not going to let me leave. I took in their sharp eyes, the rocks clutched in their paws or lying next to piles of discarded shells.

I was going to have to flee for my life.

But then I remembered Tristan and my pups, and a steely resolve replaced my fear. I was not leaving here without the amethyst. My eyes darted around the cave, taking in all the shelves, all the tools. Surely the otters wouldn't just hide something so important with a bunch of tools... Oh.

Oh!

My eyes slid over to Murray, who sat next to me with his arms crossed tightly. He scowled when he caught me looking, but I held his gaze, heart pounding rapid-fire in my chest.

Rocks were the most important tools in the ocean, Murray had said. And the otters didn't keep them on shelves. They kept them in their arm pouches.

But Murray hadn't taken his special rock out.

A buzzing sound filled my ears. I looked at the giant squid centerpiece, and then at Priscilla's rock, which lay next to Murray's plate. It was flat, and one end was fairly sharp. Not as sharp as a knife, but sharp enough to cut.

I can't do that. I can't. I can't.

I swallowed hard, trying to steel myself for what

I knew I had to do. *I won't actually hurt him,* I swore silently. *I won't. I'll just frighten him. All I need is the element of surprise. Just a few seconds.*

"That was a wonderful story, Priscilla," I said, my voice breaking the quiet. "You told it much better than I could have. Only…I have an even better ending."

And without a moment's hesitation, I snatched up Priscilla's knife and lunged at Murray, letting out a primal scream that I hoped sounded more fierce than frightened. The sea otter's eyes zeroed in on the sharp edge of the rock, and he threw his arms up to protect himself. As I landed on him, I let go of the rock and shoved my hand into the exposed pouch under his armpit.

My fingers closed around something small and hard and smooth, and I yanked it out and pulled back.

"*No!*"

Murray let out a furious snarl and threw himself at me. I felt his nails scratch a deep gouge in my arm as I lurched back. Every sea otter shot up out of their seats, and I knew I had only one chance to escape. Raising my arms, I focused with all my might on channeling every bit of power I had—and I sent it right to the squid centerpiece.

POOF!

Black ink bloomed in the water like a silent explosion. Chaos broke out as the sea otters swam blindly, some yelling, others screaming. I sped through the ink cloud, aiming for the cave's exit.

I didn't even look at the thing clenched in my palm as I swam for my life. The sea otters were shouting and swearing behind me, and I knew they'd followed me out of the cave—the ink cloud had only bought me a few seconds of extra time. Hopefully it was enough.

But no matter how hard I swam, I couldn't seem to shake them. Finally, I chanced a glance over my shoulder and nearly screamed at how close they were—and they were gaining on me. *Fast.*

Foolish, foolish girl, I thought frantically, pumping all eight tentacles as hard as I could as I shot up toward the cliff. Why had I ever thought I could outswim them? They were born in the water, and I had barely been allowed to dip my toe in the ocean; I was new at this; I didn't have a chance and the cliff was too far away; they were going to catch me and tear me limb from limb; it was completely hopeless...

HOOOOOONK!

Startled, I glanced to the right and saw Mac's beady black eyes peering out from a crevasse. I swerved hard and fast and heard the otters whoosh past me.

"Hurry, Violet!" Mac yelped as he backed up, giving me room to enter. I barely had time to think about the fact that the sea otters could easily fit through this crevasse too before I was inside.

"They're right behind me," I gasped as my eyes adjusted to the darkness. I spotted Mac behind a giant rock and, for a second, I thought he was hiding (and doing a really terrible job of it, since I could totally see him). But then he shoved the rock forward and I caught on to his plan.

"Let me help!"

I joined him, and together we heaved and pushed the rock until it finally rolled into place, blocking the crevasse closed.

I struggled to catch my breath as the otters pounded and hollered and wailed on the other side of the rock. Murray's voice cut through above the rest, although it took a few seconds for me to understand what he was saying.

"How could you? How *could* you?"

My shoulders sank, and I took a deep breath. The sea otters had been so kind, so welcoming, and I had just betrayed them in the worst possible way.

"I guess you found the amethyst?" Mac asked.

I blinked. I hadn't even looked at the amethyst yet. Mac moved closer, and slowly, I opened my palm. A bright purple gem the exact same color as my eyes gleamed in my palm, and my breath caught in my throat.

"Yeah," I whispered. "I guess I did."

Mac smiled. "One down, two to go!"

"Right."

Carefully, I tucked the amethyst into my pocket along with the pearl. Then I followed Mac into the darkness of the crevasse, trying my best to ignore the awful guilt eating away at my insides. This was a victory, but it didn't feel like one. Not at all.

I was helping a sea witch. A serpent.

I'll make it up to you, Murray, I promised silently, tears burning behind my eyes. *I'll make it up to everyone. I'm not a villain.*

I'm not a villain.

I'm not a villain.

Mac hummed happily as he led me out of the crevasse and into brighter waters. I tried to pretend I was in a good mood, too. After all, I'd found one of the three gems. I was one step closer to saving Tristan and Flotsam and Jetsam.

I was also one step closer to unleashing an evil witch on the ocean and all of the wonderful creatures that inhabited it.

"You look blue," Mac said, nudging me gently. "I mean, not literally blue. You look sad."

I pressed my lips together tightly before responding. "It's just that I don't know where to begin finding the other two gems," I said slowly. "I acted rashly with the sea otters. If whoever cast this curse on Hydra gave one of the gems to the sea otters, maybe they knew where the other two were hidden, too! I should have tried reasoning with them. Instead, I just…attacked."

Mac looked slightly offended. "My mum says that's the best way to get what you want. *ATTAAAAACK*!" he roared, zooming up ahead and sending a school of fish scattering. He turned back to face me with a hopeful smile, and I tried to smile back.

"I suppose. I mean, it *was* effective. And there's probably no way Murray would've handed the amethyst over, no matter how much I tried to reason with him."

"That's the spirit! Hey, why don't we rest for a minute?" Mac suggested. "We've been swimming for a while, and we don't even know where we're going!"

"Yeah, good idea."

I settled onto a mossy rock, while Mac floated a few feet away. Taking out the amethyst, I cupped it in my palm and studied it closely. It really was an extraordinary shade of purple; it almost seemed to glow from within. The cut was triangular with rounded points.

I frowned slightly. Something about this gem was niggling at the back of my mind, like an itch I couldn't quite scratch.

"I almost feel like I've seen this before," I told Mac. "I mean, I definitely haven't, but…I don't know, it's weird. Like déjà vu."

"You said your cousin told you stories about it," Mac said. "Maybe he just described it so well, you feel like you've seen it before."

"Yeah," I murmured. But I knew deep down that whatever this feeling was, it had nothing to do with Tristan's story.

"Hey, are you hungry?"

I glanced up to see Mac watching me with a hopeful expression. "Yes," I admitted, remembering the magnificent shellfish feast. "I ate with the sea otters. I was going to bring you something, but... well..."

"But then you stole the amethyst and they all wanted to kill you," Mac said cheerfully. "No worries. Do you mind if I go grab a quick bite?"

"Of course not! I'll stay right here."

I smiled at Mac as he swam out of sight. In all honesty, I was glad for an excuse to rest longer. I had no idea where to go from here, and I was still exhausted from the chase. My arm had finally stopped bleeding, but the cut was really stinging.

Still gripping the amethyst, I pulled the shell compact from my pocket. I opened it and gazed at my purple eyes in the mirror.

"Tristan? Can you hear me?"

I waited, even though I knew nothing would happen. Then, to my surprise, my reflection shimmered and vanished, replaced with…

"Tristan!" I shouted, beaming at him. "Remember that story about the amethyst and the sea otters? I *found* it, look!"

I held the gem up for him to see. But my excitement was quickly replaced with dread when I noticed Tristan's expression. He looked terrified.

"Violet, stop, this was all a trick!"

"What?"

"The mirrors!" Tristan said. He sounded so desperate it nearly broke my heart. "Hydra *wanted* us to communicate because it gave her a way to spy on you!"

The shock only lasted for a moment. Then I shrugged, attempting to look brave. "So what? I'm doing exactly what she asked. I'm getting the gems."

"Listen, Violet, it's all a trap. Don't come back for me."

I stared at my cousin in disbelief. "Tristan, I am not leaving you and Flotsam and Jetsam in that trench with Hydra. No way."

"But if you give her the gems—"

"I know what will happen, and I don't care!" I said, my voice rising to a hysterical pitch. "I'm not leaving you to die!"

"Violet, please…don't…"

His voice faded, and a moment later, Tristan was gone.

I snapped the compact shut, more afraid and frustrated than ever. So, Hydra had been spying. I meant what I'd said to Tristan. It didn't matter! I was fetching the gems, just like Hydra wanted. He couldn't possibly think I would just leave him and my pups down at the bottom of the ocean forever, did he?

Unsettled, I pocketed the compact and tried to focus on the remaining gems. Blood bloomed from the cut on my arm, and I waved at it until it dissipated in the water.

I stared at the cut for a moment, frowning. What was it Hydra had said, when I'd asked her how I was supposed to find the gems?

Just follow your instincts, my dear. It's in your blood.

My blood.

What had she meant by that? Was she referring to my family? No, that couldn't be. Then it dawned on me. *Your instincts, your blood*...she meant my *powers*.

Maybe I didn't have to find the gems. Maybe I could use my powers to summon the gems to *me*!

I exhaled slowly, watched the bubbles stream from my mouth. Gripping the amethyst tightly, I closed my eyes and focused as hard as I could on the other gems.

Or at least, I tried to. But it was hard to focus on

them, seeing as how I had no idea what they actually looked like.

"Okay, forget that," I said out loud. Instead, I pictured the amethyst. And almost right away, that niggling feeling was back, the feeling that I'd seen it before. Or seen something like it. I frowned, examining the thought further. A ring...an amethyst ring? I'd never seen one before, and yet I could envision the purple gem set into a gold band, and—

Something grazed my arm, and my eyes flew open. I realized the net was closing around me a split second too late.

"What?" I gasped, flying off the rock and twisting around, trying to see. That was a mistake; my tentacles got tangled in the net as it closed tightly and began pulling me up to the surface.

"Help! *Mac, help me!*" I screamed as loudly as I could, clawing at the net in terror. Tilting my head back, I saw the outline of a ship in the distance, and my stomach flipped over. If anyone from Elsinore saw me like this, with octopus tentacles, able to breathe underwater...

Who cares. The voice in my head was cold and angry. *Who cares if they think you're a witch. They should fear you. You're powerful. You could destroy them all.*

It wasn't Hydra's voice, but my own. And that was somehow more frightening to me than anything else that had happened. What was happening to me?

"Mac! Mac, *help*!" I called again, and to my relief, the baby shark appeared not too far below me.

"Violet! Hang on, I'm coming!"

Mac raced toward me as fast as he could swim, and I could see even from a distance that he was frantic with fear.

The net surged upward with renewed speed, and I let out a shriek. "Hurry!"

Mac reached me at last, and his slashed and bit at the ropes with his teeth, just barely missing my skin. The ropes began to fray slightly, but we were nearly at the surface now.

"Mac, please," I begged, and the baby shark bit onto the net and shook his head vigorously. But the ropes still wouldn't give, and then suddenly, we broke the surface.

I gasped as fresh air hit my skin for the first time in over a day. "Go, get away from the ship!" I said hastily, pushing Mac away from the net. "I'll be fine. Save yourself!"

Mac's eyes brimmed with tears, but he let go of the net and plunged back into the ocean. I watched him sink beneath the waves, then gasped as the net was hauled up and over the side of the ship. I flew through the air and watched the world tilt, sky below me and sea above me, the ship's sails rotating in a full circle—and then I landed hard on the wooden

167

planks.

The landing knocked the wind out of me, and I lay there, my tentacles twitching, listening at the sound of footsteps clunking toward me. I would fight. I would tear this ship apart. This fisherman would regret making me his catch of the day. If I had to, I would...

A pair of dusty, all too familiar boots stopped in front of me. I stopped breathing. No. It couldn't be.

Then, slowly, I tilted my head back and gazed up into the hardened, wrinkled face of the King of Elsinore.

"Grandfather," I whispered.

15

TRUTH

Moments before, I was ready to fight for my life. But the look on Grandfather's face drained all of the fight out of me.

It wasn't like back at my birthday party, where the sight of the silver streak in my hair had given him a shock. Now, he was staring down at the tentacles sprawled around me instead of legs...and he didn't look surprised at all. Nor did he look afraid.

He looked angry.

His ice-blue eyes were narrowed, the pupils tiny black pinpoints, the furry white brows pulled down in a narrow V-shape. His mouth was in a taut grimace, a muscle twitching in his sun-weathered cheek.

Elsinore had been enjoying a time of peace since before I was born. But I had heard tales of Grandfather's heroic actions during the war against the Dark Ones decades ago. I had grown up imagining him in battle, staring fearlessly into the face of his enemy.

And now that was me. I was the enemy.

I am not a villain, I wanted to say. But my mouth couldn't seem to form words anymore. One of my tentacles jerked and flopped like a dying fish. Grandfather's lip curled in disgust, and it cut through me like a knife, the hurt sharp and searing.

"I can explain," I finally managed to say, and I reached into my pocket. My fingers fumbled around the two stones, feeling for the pearl, but I was trembling now, and I pulled out the amethyst by mistake. Upon seeing the purple gem, Grandfather made a low, growling sound that was more animal than human.

"So, it's true, then," he hissed, and I shrank away from him. "You're actually helping that sea witch. You've betrayed your family and your kingdom."

"What are you talking about?" But my confusion only lasted a moment. "Your pact with Poseidon… the curse, the one Mother said I was a part of…it's the same curse, isn't it. *You* cursed Hydra. You and Poseidon."

But Grandfather seemed not to hear me at all. His

eyes were wide now, unfocused and almost wild-looking, as if he wasn't looking at me, but *through* me.

"I did everything I could to stop this from happening and it still wasn't enough. I was weak. I was a fool. No more."

Suddenly, he lunged for me with his arms outstretched. For one crazy moment I thought my own grandfather was going to strangle me to death. But then he snatched the amethyst with one hand, the other hand reaching into my pocket and grabbing the pearl. My tentacles shrank and twisted together painfully, and I screamed, closing my eyes against the agony. But when I looked down again, I saw my legs—pale, bony, scabby knees and all.

"Grandfather, wait, listen," I begged, reaching for his boots. My legs were quaking, and I didn't have the strength to stand. Hot tears poured down my cheeks as Grandfather stepped away, glowering down at me. Behind him, I caught a glimpse of Sirena standing in the entrance to the main cabin. Her hands were pressed to her cheeks, her eyes wide with horror as she watched me scrabbling, groveling at the king's feet.

Shame burned inside of me. Was Cora here, too? Even if she wasn't, she would no doubt find out about this—everyone in Elsinore would know. What was Grandfather going to do with me now that I'd revealed myself to be exactly what everyone had always feared I was?

"I should have known Hydra would find a way to get to you," Grandfather was saying. His voice was hoarse and odd-sounding, a few decibels higher than normal. "I tried to destroy this pearl, but nothing could do it—not fire, not steel, not acid. And so, I hid it. I had hoped that if you ever came upon it… if you ever knew what it could do…I had hoped you wouldn't give in to the temptation. But it appears the call of the sea, the call of a sea *witch,* is too strong for you."

"She didn't tempt me, she *tricked* me!"

The words came out shrill, but I finally had his attention. Grandfather stared down at me, the precious stones clenched in his fist. And suddenly, my head cleared. I knew exactly what to say to make him understand.

"I never wanted to help Hydra. But she has Flotsam and Jetsam. And Grandfather—she has Tristan. He's *alive!*"

Sirena gasped, but Grandfather merely blinked. I fumbled for the shell compact and opened it. "Tristan? Tristan, can you hear me? Tristan, please, please answer—*ah!*"

The moment Tristan's face filled the mirror, I held it up so Grandfather could see. I watched as his eyes widened, and my heart lifted as he began to process the truth. Tristan was alive. He needed us. Grandfather and I were on the same side. Together, we would figure out a way to defeat Hydra. Grandfather would see how useful my powers could be. This was my chance to prove to him that magic could be used for good, that I wasn't some evil witch. That I could even be a hero, like him.

"Give me the pearl, Grandfather," I rasped, struggling to sit up as I held the compact mirror high. "And the amethyst, and the other two gems. I won't give them to Hydra! We can work together—we can trick *her*! But the most important thing is that we save Tristan and Flotsam and Jetsam!" When Grandfather didn't respond, I clasped my hands together and begged. "Please, *please.* She'll kill them if we don't do something!"

My words hung in the air for a long moment. I didn't dare look away from Grandfather's face. I was waiting for his expression to relax into his soft, familiar smile, for him to say, "Yes, of course you're right, Violet. Let's save them together."

But his mouth remained a thin line, and his eyes were cold as icebergs.

"They're already as good as dead."

My mouth fell open. I couldn't believe my ears. He didn't mean—he wasn't planning on—he couldn't possibly—

Protests rose up in my throat, but I seemed to have

forgotten how to form words.

"This—this witchcraft can't be trusted," Grandfather added, snatching the compact from my hand and snapping it closed. "It's a dark trick, the worst kind of magic, giving you false hope that someone you love isn't really *dead*." On that last word, he flung the compact overboard.

"*No!*" I screamed, reaching for it, but it was too late. The compact hit the water with a distant splash, and just like that, my only connection to my cousin was lost to the deep.

And then Grandfather seized me by the arm and lifted me up like I was nothing more than a rag doll.

"What…" was all I managed to gasp as he whisked me past a gaping Sirena, into the main cabin, and down the stairs. I realized what he was doing a moment before he actually did it, and I clawed at his fingers around my arm, but his grip was too tight.

He shoved me into the brig and slammed the door. I threw myself at the bars, shaking them and sobbing, pleading and begging, but Grandfather didn't even look at me. He turned the key in the padlock with a loud *click,* then headed back up the stairs. A moment later, one of his guards appeared. He watched me with an impassive expression as I huddled on the floor of my cage and wept.

I cried for what must have been hours, until it felt as though every last tear had been wrung from my body.

The ship was moving, no doubt heading back to land. To Elsinore. Leaving Tristan and Flotsam and Jetsam to suffer their fates at the bottom of the ocean.

My throat ached from sobbing, but it was nothing compared to the ache in my heart. How could Grandfather do this? How could he leave his own grandson to die at the hands of a sea witch? For the last two years, he had done everything he could to protect us, and now he wasn't even going to try and save Tristan from Hydra?

Maybe Hydra isn't the enemy here, a voice whispered in my mind. *And maybe you aren't a villain, either. Maybe it was King Kronborg all along.*

I let out a loud hiccup and wiped my eyes. The guard still stood stoically by the stairs, watching me. I crawled over to the darkest corner of the brig and sat with my back against the wall, knees pulled into my chest.

He's so afraid of power, he won't fight for what's right, the voice continued. I found myself nodding along. After all, what had I done to deserve this imprisonment? I had tried to do everything I could to rescue my cousin—how was that worthy of punishment?

Another thought occurred to me, and I couldn't believe I hadn't considered it before. I had assumed that Hydra had done something awful, that she deserved to be trapped in the darkest, coldest part of the ocean. But what if she hadn't done anything wrong at all? Yes, she had kidnapped Tristan—but she hadn't hurt him. She had only done what she had to do to break the curse.

And Hydra was the only person to see my powers for what they were: a gift. She had helped me. She had led me to the pearl. If I had brought her the gems and freed her, she would have been so grateful. She would have released Tristan and my pups, and then she and I could rule the ocean together. We could show everyone that power like ours was nothing to fear.

It dawned on me suddenly that perhaps Hydra was a prisoner of the curse for the same reason I was: she had power. She hadn't done anything wrong. She had simply existed. Her prison was a cave in the deepest trench in the ocean, and mine was a castle with a giant wall.

The anger returned, swelling and building inside of me, pushing out all of the sadness and grief. I flexed my fingers, enjoying the feel of hot fury pulsing through my veins.

Not fury. Power.

I giggle escaped my lips, and the guard looked up sharply. I ignored him.

"Oh, Grandfather, you fool," I whispered. "I might need that pearl to breathe in the ocean, but I certainly don't need it to get out of this cage. Have you already forgotten what happened at my birthday party?"

"Excuse me?" The guard took a hesitant step forward, gripping the hilt of his sword. "Do you need something, my lady? Should I summon the king?"

"I was so angry at my party," I went on. My skin was so hot now, like I had a fever. "I was so sick and tired of being stared at. Of being feared. But guess what, Grandfather?"

"Miss?" The guard peered into the brig, his brows knit. I met his gaze and smiled.

"I *like* being feared."

The explosion blew the brig door clear off its hinges, sending the guard flying back into the wall. He slumped to the floor, eyes wide with shock, before his gaze slid out of focus.

Power radiated from the center of my chest. I could practically see it pulsing in the air as I got to my feet. My legs no longer shook. I felt strong. I felt invincible.

I left the brig, stepped over the guard's unconscious body, and headed up the stairs. I could hear shouts coming from the main cabin, and I knew Grandfather must have heard the explosion.

Good. Let him try and stop me.

But when the door at the top of the stairs flew open, it was not Grandfather standing there. It was Sirena.

I paused, eyeing the chef. Her round face was determined, but I could see the fear in her eyes. She wielded a rolling pin like a weapon, and I almost laughed.

"Violet, sweetheart," she said quietly. "Please, please listen to me. I know you're upset, but—"

"You really think I'm the enemy here, don't you."

Sirena blinked. "Sorry?"

I shook my head. "Grandfather has you all fooled. He has you convinced I'm the villain, that I deserve to be locked up. He should take a closer look at who he trusts and who he doesn't." I thought of Emil and let out a cold laugh. "Like his advisor. He's planning a coup. Does the king know?"

"What?" Sirena's face paled. "Ar-are you talking about Emil?"

"Yes, but it doesn't matter, does it?" I said with a shrug. "I almost hope Emil succeeds. Maybe the king does need to step down. After all, he threw me in the brig like a criminal, a villain…but who's the one trying to save Tristan's life—and who's the one leaving him behind to die?"

Sirena's face crumpled, as if she was on the verge of tears. "Violet, sweetie, it's awful about Tristan, I know, but—"

Whatever excuse she was going to make for Grandfather, I wasn't about to hear it. I thrust my hands forward just as Hydra had done back in the

178

cave, sending a shimmering wave straight at Sirena. She flew backwards with a shriek, and I climbed the remaining steps and entered the main cabin.

Sirena hovered in the air, trapped in a bubble. I felt a twinge of pride at what I'd managed to do— and a tiny pinprick of shame, too.

"Violet, listen, Violet *please*..."

"Don't worry, Sirena. Emil won't overthrow the king." I smiled. "Because I'm going to beat him to it."

I left her in the main cabin and stepped out onto the deck. Grandfather stood at the bow of the ship, at least eleven of his guards between us.

Coward, I thought disdainfully. *The King of Elsinore truly is nothing more than a coward. These people deserve a* real *leader. A queen.*

I waved my arm carelessly, and the guards cried out as my power blasted them off their feet. For a moment, I considered sweeping them over the side of the ship and into the ocean. But then I took pity on them. They were only following the king's orders. It was him who needed to answer for his mistakes, and no one else.

I squeezed my hand into a fist and dropped my arm. The guards fell to the floor and lay there, stiff as boards, their eyes blink-blink-blinking in confusion.

I reveled in my strength. No castle, no wall, no guards would ever stand in between me and my freedom again. I stepped forward and watched as Grandfather's expression shifted from surprise to genuine fear.

"I am your granddaughter, not your prisoner," I told him. "I will never be a prisoner again. And neither will Tristan. You might be willing to leave him to drown, but I'm not."

"Violet, listen to me—"

"Give me the pearl."

"Violet, wait, you don't understand, let me explain…" His voice was desperate, and he kept twisting the ring on his right hand. I continued walking forward.

"Now you want to explain? I don't think so. I…"

I froze, staring at his ring. The ruby. The trilliant cut.

How had I not realized it sooner? This was why the amethyst had looked so familiar. It was cut in the same shape as Grandfather's ruby ring.

Follow your instincts. It's in your blood.

My pulse quickened as I remembered Hydra's words. The last time I'd remembered them, I was holding the amethyst in my hands, focusing on the niggling feeling of déjà vu, trying to "follow my instincts" and use my powers to find the other gems…

And that was when Grandfather's net had closed around me.

How had he found me, in the endless expanse of

the ocean? How had he known precisely where I'd be? The answer was obvious now. He hadn't known at all.

I had summoned him.

"Your ring," I said, and Grandfather looked down at his hand. Then, far too late, he hid his hand behind his back.

"Violet—"

"It's one of the three gems," I went on, my throat dry and scratchy. "You didn't just know about the curse on Hydra. You *are* the one who cursed her. You and Poseidon."

Grandfather bowed his head. I waited for him to deny it, to offer some explanation. But then he nodded, and I took a step back.

"How could you," I whispered. "What did she do? Did she do anything at all? Or was it just that you couldn't stand the thought that there was someone out there with more power than you?"

"Violet, just listen—"

"*No!*"

It felt as though an invisible claw had ripped the word from my throat. The white-hot rage pulsing at the center of my chest exploded, sending Grandfather flying backwards. As he hit the bow, I swiped the air with my hand. The ruby ring flew off his finger, and the amethyst and the pearl slipped out of his grip. I caught all three easily, then stalked forward until I stood right in front of his cowering form.

"Violet," Grandfather said again. "Hydra isn't who you think."

I said nothing, only glowered at him. But this time, I didn't cut him off. Because now I was remembering Priscilla's tale of the two kings, the marriage of land and sea, and something about it was nagging at me. I waited for Grandfather to continue.

"The Dark Ones…they were taking over," Grandfather said hoarsely. "Poseidon and I needed the most powerful curse to stop them. But they heard of our plans, and they came up with a plan of their own."

My breathing had gone ragged as I listened intently.

"The Dark Ones had a child," he whispered. "A baby they kept secret. We didn't learn of her existence until after we had destroyed her family."

Destroyed her family.

No.

It couldn't be.

"The curse had trapped her in the trench where the Dark Ones dwelled," Grandfather said, barely audible now. "But they had enacted a counter curse of their own. A way for the child to break free of the curse."

"The gems," I said quietly, and he nodded.

"Poseidon and I tracked them down. We hid them,

kept them safe. Or so we thought. We only had to hide them until the marriage of land and sea could take place."

My eyes widened as I remembered Mother's words in the letter. *She must be allowed to choose her own path, to make her own choices.* "That's the part of the curse that includes me?" I asked softly.

Grandfather lifted his eyes to meet mine. "Yes. Poseidon...he has a son your age. His name is Triton."

He fell quiet, his gaze pleading with me to understand. And I did.

"I'm to marry Triton one day, and that will cement the curse."

"Yes."

"The curse that will keep Hydra permanently in the trench."

"Yes."

"Because Hydra is the last of the Dark Ones," I said, and Grandfather nodded again. "You destroyed her family. You kept her trapped in a trench when she was a *baby.* When she had done nothing wrong except to exist."

"Violet, she was a Dark One, she's a vi—"

"She's only a villain because you *made her one*," I screamed, and Grandfather flinched. I stepped closer and hissed: "And you made me one, too."

With that, I squeezed the pearl. Warmth rushed

through me, and I felt my legs split into tentacles, which thrashed against the deck and caused Grandfather to cry out in fear.

"Violet…w-where did you get that?"

I realized he was pointing at my chest, and I looked down. Mother's opal necklace hung there, black and glistening in the sun.

Our eyes met, and suddenly, everything clicked into place.

Grandfather swallowed visibly. "Sweetheart, listen to me, please, you mustn't—"

But I was done listening. I leaped over the side of the boat and plunged into the blissfully cool ocean. The water felt like pure bliss, and I marveled at how the sea felt like home, like I was always meant to be here.

I began to swim as fast as I could toward the trench. There was no sign of Mac anywhere, but that was probably for the best—he was sweet, but also a bit of a coward, and what I was about to do was incredibly dangerous. I couldn't ask him to come.

This time, I was making the journey to Hydra on my own.

16

THE DARK ONE

My fury at Grandfather gradually faded from a boil to a simmer as the water grew chillier and chillier. And while I was still angry at Hydra for tricking me and taking my cousin and my pups hostage, I couldn't help feeling bad for her, too. She was a victim, like me. She hadn't done anything wrong other than to be herself, to have powers.

Yet when she was only a baby, Grandfather had imprisoned her in a place so dark, light itself couldn't break through. It was so cruel.

He was cruel. Just like Mac said. But more than that, he was a coward.

I knew I could explain this to Hydra. I would

reason with her, and she would understand. Whatever revenge on Grandfather she had been plotting all this time in her cave, I could convince her to let go of it. I would give her the gems, we would destroy them together and break the curse, and she would return my loved ones.

We were on the same side. I would make her understand that.

And yet, as I drew closer to her cave, something was bothering me. It felt like an itch I couldn't quite scratch. I landed outside the entrance to the cave and hesitated for a moment, thinking hard. Then an achingly familiar voice reached my ears.

"Violet? Is that you?"

My heart stopped, and I let out a cry as I rushed into the cave. The green glow was slightly dimmer, and I half-expected Hydra to appear, blocking my way. But there was no sign of the sea witch. I moved around the cauldron, looking around expectantly, but the cave was empty.

"No, no, no," I murmured, trying to focus. I had heard my cousin's voice. He was here, and so were my pups. This was a trick, that was all. And I wasn't going to fall for it.

For a moment, I stood there with my eyes closed. Then I turned slowly to face the wall to my right. The wall that had shimmered ever so slightly the last time I'd been here.

I moved closer, studying the wall. When I reached it, I saw up close that the rock didn't quite look like the rest of the cave. It was ever so slightly translucent.

Holding my breath, I reached out to touch the wall—and my hand slid straight through as if it was nothing more than a bit of sea foam.

A mirage. I stepped through it without hesitation, heart pounding in my ears.

This cavern was smaller, with sickly pink flowers dangling from the ceiling and growing in patches from the floor. A vanity desk sat on one side, tubes of lipstick and jars of powder crowded in front of the oval-shaped mirror. But my gaze went right to the other side of the cave, to the two bubbles floating there, waiting for me. Inside the one on the right, Flotsam and Jetsam wagged their tails furiously at the sight of me. And inside the one on the left was...

"Tristan!" I cried, hurrying over to him. I just barely managed to stop myself in time from throwing myself at the bubble and getting knocked back like last time.

Tristan smiled wanly at me. He was thin and pale and tired-looking, but he was alive. He was *alive.* Once again, I thought about how Grandfather was ready to leave him down here in this cave, and I felt another surge of rage.

"I like the tentacles," Tristan said jokingly. "I tried to tell you the first time, but you couldn't hear me."

It took a moment for me to understand what he meant. "You...you were here?" I sputtered. "You were here when Hydra took Flotsam and Jetsam?"

Tristan nodded sadly. "I could see through the mirage," he said with a sigh. "I think Hydra did it on purpose just to torture me. I was shouting your name the whole time, but I guess this little cavern is soundproof. I knew she was going to trick you—I tried to warn you the next time we talked with the compact mirrors. I'm so sorry, Violet."

All thoughts of forgiving Hydra flew from my mind. Tristan had been right there in the cave, and I had been clueless. Hydra had lied to me from the beginning, when she'd shown me the sunken ship in her bubble. Maybe we weren't the same after all. Maybe she was just an evil sea witch, the last surviving Dark One, who deserved to be cursed.

The itch returned, stronger than ever—a thought trying to surface, but it couldn't quite seem to fully form. *Why?* I kept thinking. *Why* had Hydra lied? But the answer was simple: she wanted me to find the gems. She wanted me to help her break the curse.

Still, something was off. But I didn't have time to sit here and ponder it now.

"I'm going to get all of you to the surface," I said to Tristan. "Then I'll use my powers to pop the bubbles. Do you know how long Hydra will be gone?"

Tristan swallowed. "She hasn't gone anywhere,

Violet. She can't leave the trench. Remember?"

A chill raced up my spine, and I mentally berated myself for being so foolish.

"Why didn't you contact me before you came down here?" Tristan asked, holding up the compact mirror.

I thought of Grandfather's face when he had seen Tristan in the mirror. Then I pictured him tossing the compact into the ocean, leaving his own grandson to his fate, and a fresh pang of anger and sorrow ripped through me. I couldn't tell Tristan the truth. I just couldn't.

"I lost it," I lied. "But it's fine. I have something much better."

I pulled the amethyst and the ruby ring from my pocket as I spoke, and Tristan's eyes went wide.

"You...you found them?" He got to his feet, moving as close to me as he could. "Violet, no, don't give them to her. "She lied. I was never on a ship. Don't you get it? It's a trap. She—"

"I know it's a trap," I said, looking around the empty cave. "But Grandfather trapped her first." I turned away from Tristan. "I don't blame you, Hydra. I understand why you did what you did. I want to help you."

"No, Violet, the ship, she sent you to the *SS Lydian* to find—"

"Hush, now," came a low voice, and I froze.

Tristan's mouth kept moving, but I couldn't hear a word he was saying. Behind his bubble, Hydra stepped out of the shadows and into view. I faced her with my head held high.

"Did you fulfill your end of the bargain, my dear?"

Tristan was shouting now, shaking his head wildly, but I ignored him.

"I did." I held out my hand so she could see the amethyst and the ruby ring glittering in my palm.

Hydra's eyes flashed with hunger. She plucked them from my hand, a slow smile curving her lips. "Oh, very good, my dear. Very good. I suppose the sea otters put up quite the fight?"

"They did." I held out my arm so she could see the gouge Murray had left on my arm. It had already started to scab over, and it throbbed and itched like mad.

Hydra looked amused. "And the great and powerful king?"

My chest tightened at the memory. "It was easy to get it off his finger. He didn't fight at all. In fact, he begged, like a coward."

Hydra threw her head back and laughed. I didn't dare look at Tristan. I couldn't imagine what he thought of me, speaking about Grandfather that way. But he had no idea that Grandfather had been prepared to leave him to die.

"I underestimated you, my dear." Hydra seemed

pleased. "This is very impressive. And now, if you please...the third gem."

She held out her hand, her eyes moving to the chain around my neck. My hand went instinctively to the opal beneath my top. I had realized, on the deck of Grandfather's ship, that the opal was the third gem. He had given it to my mother to keep safe, and that was why she had never taken it off.

But now the itch was back, and the question my mind had been trying to ask finally surfaced. *Why had mother hidden the opal right before she died?*

The answer was that she had known who was coming. Who was desperate enough to kill for the opal. Who needed it for her freedom.

And it wasn't Poseidon.

She sent you to the SS Lydian, Tristan had cried desperately, right before Hydra silenced him. She had kept Tristan here in this cave all along, but she had tricked me into thinking he was on a sunken ship. And sure enough, I'd found the only ship that had sunk in the waters off the coast of Elsinore...the *SS Lydian*.

Hydra had known the gem was stashed away on my parents' ship. And there was only one way that was possible.

"You killed them."

Tristan, Flotsam, and Jetsam went perfectly still in their bubbles. Hydra studied me, her smile fading.

Her eyes glinted like coins.

"You killed my parents," I whispered again. "That's what Grandfather was trying to tell me before I jumped off the ship. That's why he kept me locked up. He wasn't afraid of my powers. He was afraid of *yours*."

My hands were beginning to shake. I couldn't forgive Grandfather, not yet. But at least now I understood where his fear was coming from. The last surviving Dark One, a sea witch he had cursed, had still managed to drown his daughter and son-in-law. I was obsessed with the sea, and I had powers. Of course, he was terrified. He really had just been trying to protect me—not just from Hydra, but from the truth.

"How could you?" I said, my voice wobbling. "My parents had done nothing to you."

Hydra rolled her eyes. "My dear, it was never my intent to kill them. I merely sent a little whirlpool up to the surface. It's not my fault your father couldn't properly captain his vessel."

Lights danced in front of my eyes, and for a moment, I was afraid I would faint.

"I had no choice," Hydra went on. "Your mother had one of the gems. And, well, if the king's daughter happened to drown...I can't deny I relished the pain that loss brought him."

A choked sob escaped me. I squeezed my hands

into fists. *Anger,* I told myself over and over again. *Anger is power.*

"And now, so your mother's death won't be in vain...I'll take that opal now, if you please."

Hydra waved her hand, and I felt her power tug hard at the necklace. But I threw my hand up, met her power with my own and pushed it away. She stepped back, eyes wide with surprise.

"My mother died protecting this gem," I said in a low voice. "She died to stop you from escaping. I am not about to let you have it."

Hydra blinked. Then she began to laugh harder than ever.

"Oh, my dear girl, I *did* underestimate you!" she exclaimed. "You're a feisty one. Quite a bit braver than your grandfather, that's for sure. You would make a decent queen...that is, if you lived long enough to see your coronation."

Before I could blink, she threw her arms up. The blast of power lifted me off my feet, and I slammed into the wall of the cave.

Bright spots danced in my eyes as I slumped to the ground, then struggled to stand. With one hand, I clutched the opal, and with the other, I threw a blast of power aimlessly.

"Careful, now," came Hydra's voice. "You almost lost your pups."

I let out a cry and looked over at the bubbles.

Tristan stood in one, gazing at me with silently pleading eyes, while Flotsam and Jetsam barked up a storm in the other. If their bubbles popped, they would drown in front of me, a thought that made my knees weak with terror.

Hydra swiped for the necklace, and I let out a scream of rage as I thrust out my free hand. This time, my aim was true, and the blast sent Hydra flying up, up, up to the ceiling of the cave and the hanging stalactites, their pointy ends like knives.

A split-second before she would have been impaled, I let my hand drop. Hydra fell to the ground with a *thud*.

I stood there, trying to catch my breath, watching her attempt to collect herself. *You could have killed her,* the voice in my head whispered, sounding awed. *You could have killed her, but you didn't.*

I don't want to kill her, I told the voice. *I just want to stop her.*

But deep down, I was already wondering if I had made a mistake.

Hydra's shoulders were shaking, and for a weird moment, I thought she was crying. Then, as she got to her feet, I saw she was laughing again.

"So powerful, and yet so weak," she said, facing me. "You should have killed me when you had the chance, dear. But you held back. Now you've lost the element of surprise." She grinned, baring her sharp teeth. For the first time, I saw Hydra's hair unravel on her head. The black and white buns she had pulled up high on her head were now venomous snakes with emerald green eyes hissing and lunging toward me. She is not only a witch—she's a sea serpent. "And I don't hold back."

She sent another, stronger blast of power at me, and I barely managed to leap out of the way in time. Behind me, a giant stalactite cracked, then began to topple over—its pointy end heading right for Flotsam and Jetsam's bubble.

"No!" I screamed, thrusting both hands forward. The stalactite slowed its fall until it came to a halt, teetering in the air at an unnatural angle, the tip just inches from my terrified pups.

I stood there panting, trembling from the effort of holding the massive rock in the air with my powers. My arms shook as I chanced a glance at Hydra. She stood next to Tristan's bubble, her smile wider than ever.

"Now, my dear," she said. "Hand over the opal, or you can watch your cousin drown."

I struggled under the weight of the stalactite. "I... you can't..."

Sighing, Hydra lifted her arm. "Oh, I can. Believe me."

Tristan was shaking his head wildly, yelling something I couldn't hear. Four words, over and over again. After a moment, I understood. *She'll drown me anyway.*

I stifled a sob. He was right. Even if I gave Hydra the opal, she would still kill Tristan. She would kill us all.

"Okay," I said meekly. Hydra's eyes flickered ember in the dim green light. "Okay, you win. Here."

And with all my remaining strength, I flung the stalactite at her, pointy end first.

Hydra's scream of pain was awful, and I looked away as she slammed into the wall. I hurried over to the bubbles and took out the pearl, squeezing it as hard as I could. It glowed bright white, surrounding all four of us like a protective shield.

At that moment, the bubbles popped.

I let out a shriek of surprise as, for just a moment, Tristan and my poor sweet pups flailed in the water. But then Flotsam and Jetsam's fur turned slick and black and their eyes glowed yellow. And Tristan...

"I have a tail!" he exclaimed, staring down at the shimmery green scales covering what had moments ago been his legs. Then he looked at me, wide-eyed. "Whoa, I can talk! I can *breathe*! Violet, I'm breathing underwater!"

My laughter sounded more like a sob. "Let's go home," I said, gesturing to the front of the cave. But we'd only made it a few feet when Hydra spoke up, her voice weak.

"You *are* a coward, just like your grandfather."

Bristling, I turned to face her—and then immediately wished I hadn't. The knife-sharp tip of the stalactite had pierced through her shoulder, pinning her to the cave wall. Blood trickled down her front, and I could see her struggling to push the rock off of her, to no avail.

"I'm nothing like my grandfather," I said in a low voice. "And I'm nothing like you. I don't kill people to get what I want."

Hydra's laugh sound like glass shattering. "Is that so? What are you doing right now, if not leaving me to die after getting what *you* want?"

"I had no choice!" I yelled. "You kidnapped my cousin—I wasn't going to let him die!"

"Do you think *I* had a choice, you foolish brat?" Hydra screamed back at me. "Your grandfather confined me to this cave, alone in the dark! I might as well be dead!"

I opened my mouth, then closed it, defeated. She was right, after all. If I left her here to die alone, I was no better than her *or* Grandfather.

I flexed my fingers, ignoring the feeling of dread creeping up my spine. Then, with a flick of my wrist, I pulled the stalactite from Hydra's shoulder and sent it flying across the cave.

Hydra slumped to the ground with a groan, hair falling in her eyes.

197

"Let's go, quickly," I said in a low voice. Tristan nodded, and we swam out of the cave with Flotsam and Jetsam flanking us.

"You did the right thing, Violet," Tristan said. "It would've been wrong to let her die like that."

"I know, but—"

I choked, grabbing frantically at my neck. For a moment, I thought a fish had swum down my throat and lodged there, cutting off my breath. Tristan was yelling my name frantically and the pups were barking like crazy. My fingers grappled with the chain of my mother's necklace, which was pulled taut against my neck. I didn't have to turn around to know Hydra was in the cave entrance, using every bit of power she had to pull the opal toward her.

I tried desperately to think. I had the pearl— if Tristan, Flotsam, and Jetsam were outside of its protective bubble, they would drown. I couldn't let Hydra pull me away from them. But I couldn't let them have the pearl, because then *I* would drown— and Hydra would surely kill them. The only other option...

Stars exploded behind my eyes, and then a different sort of darkness began to creep in on the edges of my vision. I knew I only had moments before I blacked out, and I had to save Tristan and my pups. I hadn't come this far to lose everything now. Desperately, I found the necklace clasp and undid it, then drew in a great, sucking breath of air as the chain flew off and the pressure released.

"Violet! Are you okay?" Tristan's concerned face swam in my vision as I massaged my neck. I turned around just as my mother's opal necklace landed in Hydra's outstretched hand.

"Oh, no," I whispered. "What have I done?"

"You didn't have a choice," Tristan reassured me. "But we can talk about that later. We need to get as far away from her as possible."

"Right."

We swam hard and fast, soaring over the edge of the cliff and aiming straight up for the surface. As the water changed from midnight blue to turquoise, I chanced a glance below us. It might have been my imagination, but I thought I saw an electric green crackling way, way down deep, and a shiver ran through me.

What evil had I just unleashed on the ocean? On the world?

17

WHIRLPOOL

By the time we broke the surface, sucking in deep lungfuls of briny air, it was obvious something was very, very wrong.

We hadn't seen a single creature the entire journey up, and now I could see a flock of seagulls disappearing along the horizon. They were fleeing. They knew something awful was coming.

And it was all my fault.

Suddenly, I remembered the dream I'd had the night before my birthday, which felt like a lifetime ago. That vision of the magnificent creature rising up out of the ocean on the distance. The sight had filled me with awe at the time, but now cold dread slithered over my bones like snakes.

"There's Grandfather's ship," Tristan said, pushing his sopping wet hair out of his eyes with one hand and pointing with the other. I spotted the ship in the distance and nodded.

"Stay close, all three of you," I said, and my pups squeezed in at my sides. Focusing all my power on the water surrounding us, I summoned the current and directed it at the ship.

"Whoa!" Tristan cried as a massive wave swelled up around us, carrying us higher and higher and faster and faster. I couldn't help but grin as Tristan whooped and laughed. "This is like flying!" he yelled, and I felt a surge of pride and love. At least one person appreciated my powers.

At least I still had one family member who loved me.

As we drew closer to the ship, seawater spraying our faces and our hair whipping in the wind, I allowed the current to slow. The wave slowed with it, but the water level remained high, carrying us the rest of the way like a gentle blue hand. On the deck, I saw Sirena scream and point. Grandfather turned around, his eyes wide with shock as the ocean gently set me, Tristan, Flotsam, and Jetsam down in front of him. I tucked the pearl back into my pocket as the water receded, grabbing Tristan's arm so he didn't topple to the floor on his weak legs. My own legs shook beneath me as they reformed, but I kept my balance.

"Hello, Grandfather," I said coolly.

The king just stood there, pale and shaking. But Sirena rushed forward, scooping Tristan up in her arms and squeezing him so tightly he laughed.

"Okay, okay," he said, sounding embarrassed.

"You're alive! I can't believe it. We thought we'd lost you forever," Sirena said, half-laughing, half-weeping as she hugged him. Grandfather and I continued to stare at one another. I knew he was wondering if I'd told Tristan that Grandfather had intended to leave him to his fate with Hydra. I wasn't about to relieve him of that anxiety.

"Violet," he said quietly, and his voice was so sad, so broken and raw, that all of the rage I'd been carrying just disappeared. He didn't look like the great King of Elsinore right now. He didn't look like a hero or a villain. He just looked like my grandfather, bereaved and worried and exhausted.

"Grandfather," I whispered, and as he opened his arms, I ran to him.

But I never made it into his embrace.

The ship gave an almighty lurch, as if a giant hand had thrust up out of the ocean directly beneath us. I screamed as I went skidding down the deck, which was suddenly almost vertical to the water. Grandfather let out a roar, and I heard Sirena and Tristan calling out too, but I couldn't see any of them, I was toppling towards the ocean—

"*Oof!*" At the last moment, I grabbed the railing and held on for dear life. My legs sailed over the side of the ship, then my body whipped back and slammed against the other side of the railing. I hung there helplessly, staring down at the water churning below…the water which was now an eerie electric green.

"Oh, no," I whispered. "She's here."

The air crackled with static, and the hairs along my arms and neck rose up. I scrabbled to gain a foothold as the ship slowly righted itself. At last, I managed to climb up over the railing. I fell hard to the deck, gasping for breath.

The crewmen were running around frantically, adjusting the sails and preparing the ship for a storm. But this was no regular storm. My gaze fell on Grandfather, who was near the mast. He had one arm around Sirena's waist, and he held Tristan over his other shoulder. His eyes met mine, and I saw my relief reflected in his expression. He had saved them both from being swept overboard.

"It's Hydra," I called out over the ruckus the men were making. "She's free. It's my fault, Grandfather, I broke the curse—I never meant to give her the gems, but…"

My words were lost to the screams and shouts as the ship lurched forward, racing in a wide arc with unnatural speed. I gasped, clinging to the railing again and gazing out at the water. The electric green glow was even brighter now, and there was something up ahead, like a great black hole in the ocean…

My heart stuttered in my chest when I realized what I was looking at. A whirlpool, at least a mile wide. And our ship was already caught up in its current.

Hydra was going to drown us all, just like she did my parents.

Clouds began to roll in rapidly, sickly green-gray and flashing with lightning. They gathered overhead as if magnetically pulled to our ship.

A fear stronger than any I'd ever felt before gripped me. I couldn't move. I stood there like a statue as chaos broke out all around me, the men trying to secure the sails against the wind, Grandfather making his way to the main cabin with Tristan and Sirena as a wave crashed overboard. I saw the grim determination on his face. He would shut them up in the cabin so they wouldn't fall overboard, then attempt to steer the ship out of the whirlpool. But he knew it was a losing battle. We were all going to the bottom of the sea. Hydra's powers were too strong to fight.

Your powers are strong, too, the voice in my head whispered. *Perhaps you don't yet know your full strength.*

"It doesn't matter," I murmured, still holding on to

the railing for dear life. "I can't beat her."

How do you know unless you try?

My heart was pounding so fast, I began to feel dizzy. I tried to summon my anger at Hydra, tried to feel anything other than bone-deep terror, but I couldn't. I couldn't do it.

I wasn't strong enough for this.

Suddenly, a hoarse scream ripped through the air, a sound so inhuman that for a moment, I thought it was some sea creature rising from the deep. Then I turned and saw Grandfather.

He stood in the entrance to the main cabin, the door thrown open, one arm still tight around Tristan. But his other arm was outstretched, reaching for Sirena, who was sliding down the tilted deck.

"No!" I cried, but then the bow of the ship jerked upwards, and suddenly we were on even ground again. Sirena slid to a stop and lay there, panting.

The men fell still and silent, looking around in confusion. The ship was perfectly still and stable. But all around us, the storm and sea were still raging.

Swallowing hard, I peered over the railing, and my jaw dropped.

The ship was levitating above the churning water. And rising up out of the waves, wearing a wide smile that showed off her pointy teeth, was Hydra.

The change was astonishing: she radiated energy, her skin a glowing golden brown, a halo of light surrounding her. Once again, I couldn't help but wonder if she had chosen the path of evil, or if she had been forced into it. She was a Dark One, I reminded myself. But she had only been a baby when Poseidon and Grandfather had cursed her. She had never been given a chance to be good.

Hydra landed neatly on the deck next to Sirena, who glared up at her.

"Witch," she spat.

Hydra sighed. "It's so amusing, how you silly little people think *witch* is an insult."

Then, with a flick of her hand, she sent Sirena skidding across the deck. Grandfather roared in fury as the chef slammed into the mast and fell still.

I clapped my hands to my mouth to stifle my cry. Hydra didn't even spare me a glance. Her attention was all on Grandfather.

He left Tristan in the entrance of the main cabin and strode toward Hydra, unsheathing his sword as he did, and all of a sudden, I wondered how I had ever called him a coward. I had my chance to kill Hydra down in the cave, and I hadn't done it.

But the expression on Grandfather's face told me that he would not throw his chance away. He would kill Hydra or die trying.

Grandfather broke into a run, sword drawn. But Hydra dodged his blow easily, laughing as she did. As he swiveled around to face her, she summoned a sword of her own, only hers seemed to be made entirely of that electric green light.

"Come on then, old man," she sneered. "Let's see how long you last."

They began to duel, swords clanging and flashing. I raced to the cabin, where Tristan still huddled in the doorway. We clung to one another, Flotsam and Jetsam pressed up against our sides, as Grandfather fought for his life. For all our lives.

"Look at Sirena," Tristan whispered. I tore my eyes off of Grandfather and Hydra and saw the chef stirring over by the mast, then finally sitting up.

"She's okay," I said in relief. Sirena took in the duel, her round face going deathly pale. She sat up, both hands pressed to her heart as she followed Grandfather's every move, and suddenly I wondered how I'd never noticed it before. "They're in love," I said in amazement, turning to Tristan. "Grandfather and Sirena are—"

The words died on my lips because Tristan was no longer next to me.

I shot to my feet as Hydra let out a cry of triumph. She had her sword pointed at Grandfather, but her other arm was high in the air—and floating over the raging waters, mere feet from the railing of the ship, was Tristan.

"You don't mind, do you, old man?" Hydra was saying. "You were content to let him drown before."

I let go of the railing and flew towards the railing, half-running, half-falling down the deck as the ship began to tilt. Hydra's laughter and Grandfather's shouts were lost to the sound of my pulse in my ears. Tristan's eyes locked onto mine, and even as his arms flailed, his hands reaching desperately for anything to grab onto, I could see the hopelessness in his gaze as he dangled there like a puppet.

Then, swiftly and silently, he fell.

Any sound from the resulting splash as his body hit the water was lost to the wind and the shouts of the men and my own horrified scream.

I was not about to let Tristan drown. Not after all I'd gone through to rescue him from that exact fate.

Hydra would not steal him from me like she had my parents.

I leaped over the railing and plunged into the ocean. The impact was like a full-body punch, and for a moment, my vision went black as pain shot through me. Then I broke the surface and sucked in the biggest breath I could before diving back beneath the waves.

The ocean was transformed. It was as if the bright turquoise waters, the pink coral, the glittering schools of fish and other colorful creatures had all been some other world I'd explored, as distant as the moon. Now I was on an alien planet, a place made up of nothing but green fog and a thrumming, pulsing light from an unseen source and a silence more chilling than any scream.

I spun in a circle, looking for any sign of Tristan, and accidentally released a few bubbles of air when I saw the whirlpool from below the surface—a black, miles-deep funnel that crackled and sparked with green light.

I couldn't help but marvel at the full strength of Hydra's powers. And I had unleashed her.

I had doomed us all.

Desperately, I tore my gaze away from the whirlpool. I had to find Tristan before the current pulled him into that vortex and I lost him forever. I pulled out the pearl, but as I squeezed it, a chunk of wood from the ship sped toward me and slammed into my injured arm. I barely managed to stop myself from screaming as stars erupted behind my eyes. Through the haze of pain and the swirl of blood from the reopened gash, I saw the pearl drifting away fast.

As I lunged for it, movement in the corner of my eye caught my attention, and my heart leaped when I saw the shape of a boy not too far away, slowly moving toward the whirlpool. *Tristan!*

But the pearl was moving in the opposite direction. For an agonizing moment, I hovered in the water, unsure of what to do. If I tried to grab the pearl first, I might not make it to Tristan in time. But could I make it all the way to him without taking another breath?

Precious seconds ticked by, and I made my decision.

I swam furiously toward Tristan, pumping my arms and legs and wishing with all my heart that I had my tentacles instead. More pieces of Grandfather's ship went sailing past, drawn into the whirlpool. I kicked as hard as I could, saltwater stinging my eyes as I kept my focus on Tristan.

At last, I reached him. His eyes were closed, mouth slightly open, and I tried not to think about whether or not I was too late as I grabbed his arm and made my way to the surface. My lungs were on fire, the pain in my arm was agony, and the urge to inhale was getting harder and harder to fight. I wanted to cry in despair. How could I have lost the pearl? It was gone now, making its way to the bottom of the ocean, right at the moment when I needed it more than ever.

More shapes appeared in front of me, and to the sides…large shapes, and for a horrible moment I thought Hydra had blown Grandfather's ship apart and I was looking at the pieces.

Then I realized the shapes had eyes. And fins.

And razor-sharp teeth.

Tristan and I were surrounded by sharks.

18

DEBT

My heart seized up, and bright neon spots danced in my vision. I knew I couldn't hold my breath for much longer, but it didn't matter now. The blood billowing from my arm had no doubt called the sharks to us. And now they were eyeing me and Tristan in a way that clearly implied we were going to be their next feast.

I waved my free hand, trying to conjure a blast of power. But all that came out was a little shimmery wave. I was too weak for this. I wondered vaguely if I would black out before the sharks reached us. Then at least I wouldn't feel any pain.

The largest of the sharks flew forward, teeth

gnashing, and I floated there, paralyzed with fear.

"Mum, no!"

Out of nowhere, Mac shot up like a rocket between us and the sharks, and I barely managed to stop myself from crying out in relief. The largest shark—his mother, apparently—slowed and glowered at her son.

"They're fair game, Mac. Get out of my way."

"No! Violet is my friend!"

The sharks all stared at me, and Mac glanced at my legs and gave me a sharp-toothed smile. "Wow, you weren't lying. You really are a human!"

I nodded, cheeks bulging with the air I was trying desperately to hold in. Mac's eyes widened in understanding.

"Get out of the way, Mac," another shark said.

"Yeah, you softie."

"And you call yourself a great white shark!"

The other sharks, who I realized must be the cousins he'd mentioned, slowly began closing in on us, jeering and taunting Mac. Darkness crept in on the outskirts of my vision, and my lungs felt as though they were on fire. I only had seconds left. I wasn't going to make it.

"I *am* a great white shark!" Mac yelled, and his family froze, staring at him in shock. "I'm as brave as any of you! And if you don't believe me, watch this!"

And with that, Mac rushed at me and Tristan, his mouth open wide, revealing every single razor-sharp tooth in his head. *He's going to eat us in front of his family,* I thought distantly, too close to unconsciousness to feel fear or shock. And then Mac scooped us up in his mouth.

It wasn't so bad, being eaten by a shark. I couldn't even feel his teeth sinking into my flesh, couldn't see the blood surely billowing out in the water, couldn't feel my bones breaking. In fact, all I could feel was the rush of water as Mac swam up and up and up…

…and then he broke the surface.

I sucked in a huge, ragged breath, coughing uncontrollably. Next to me, Tristan's head flopped back, but he didn't move.

"Tristan," I rasped, my voice aching as I pressed over and over again on his chest. "Tristan, come on. Come *on*!"

Suddenly, Tristan's head jerked up. He lurched to the side and coughed, returning a lungful of seawater to the sea, and I went weak with relief. Tristan was breathing. He was alive. We were both alive.

"Ah ooh oh-ay?"

Mac spoke with his mouth still wide open, Tristan and I hanging out on either side. I let out a shaky laugh.

"Yes, Mac. We're okay, thanks to you."

I patted the shark's cheek, and I thought I could

feel him smile around me. It was disconcerting and comforting all at once.

We stayed like that for a few minutes, Tristan still coughing up seawater, me trying to catch my breath. I had lost the pearl. I didn't regret my choice, and I knew there were bigger things to worry about right now, but the loss still stung.

I would never be able to breathe underwater again. I would never feel the power of my tentacles propelling me effortlessly through the water. I would never know that freedom of life in the sea. A tear slid down my cheek, and I wiped it away hastily.

"Mac, do you see my grandfather's ship?"

In response, Mac swam in a slow circle. "Yeh, oh-er 'ere!" he cried, and we began to move. I couldn't see where we were going, but for the moment, I was okay with that. I lay there limply in Mac's mouth, feeling the rise and fall of Tristan's chest as he panted next to me.

"Eer!" Mac said happily. Turning my head, I saw the side of Grandfather's ship, the bottom still hovering several feet above the water. The rope ladder hung off the side, frayed and dangling in the wind. I helped Tristan out first, and he clung to the rope, his face pale with exhaustion. I grabbed onto the bottom rung, then leaned over and kissed the top of Mac's head.

"Thank you for everything, Mac," I told him,

trying not to cry. "You're the best and bravest great white shark I've ever met."

Mac sniffled loudly. "Will I ever see you again?"

I pictured the pearl vanishing into the fathoms below and tried to smile.

"I hope so."

The baby shark gave me a sad smile. "Me, too. Goodbye, Violet."

"Goodbye, Mac."

With that, I turned and began to climb up the ladder, keeping hold of Tristan's elbow. It was slow going, since Tristan had to rely entirely on the strength of his arms, and both of us were exhausted. But at last, we made it to the top and clambered over the railing.

To my astonishment, Hydra and Grandfather were still dueling. It was a fierce and furious battle, his mighty sword clashing with her rod of pure light and power, sending yellow and green sparks flying into the air. Sirena stood exactly where she had when I'd jumped off the ship, her hands clasped to her heart. Her eyes moved to where Tristan and I lay in a heap, and she let out a choked cry.

Grandfather heard her, and he looked in our direction. He faltered when he saw us, his sword freezing mid-parry, relief and joy etched into every single wrinkle on his face, and right then I loved him so much I thought I would burst into tears.

That moment of hesitation was all Hydra needed.

It happened as if in slow motion. She lunged forward, her lightning rod a brilliant flash of white-hot power that slashed across Grandfather's chest. His crystal-clear blue eyes widened, not with pain, just with surprise, as crimson red blood bloomed on his torn white shirt. He blinked once, twice.

And then the King of Elsinore fell to the deck and lay there, motionless as a rock.

My scream mingled with Sirena's, and Tristan cried out, too. Hydra threw back her head and laughed in triumph, the awful sound echoing in my ears, stirring up the rage I had felt down in the cave when I realized she had killed my parents. Only this was a fury wilder and more out-of-control than any I had ever felt before. I hadn't been able to kill Hydra then.

I would not make the same mistake again.

I rushed forward, thrusting my hands forward as I did. Hydra abruptly stopped, laughing as my power threw her back against the mast, pinning her there. She sneered at me, wriggling against her invisible bonds.

"You really think you're a match for me, little girl? The granddaughter of a cowardly king? I am a Dark One. It took the combined forces of the king of Elsinore and the king of the sea to hold me down, and I still managed to break free of their curse—"

Her words were cut off by a scream as I flicked

my wrist and smacked her head against the mast with a loud *crack*. Distantly, I heard Sirena and Tristan begging me to stop, but there was no way I could stop now even if I wanted to.

Power thrummed through me with the force of the entire ocean. I could sense every inch of the sea, the crushing weight of the water, the pulsing heartbeats of the thousands of creatures that inhabited the water, the massive whirlpool growing wider and deeper by the second. And I could feel my power reaching into all of it like millions of tendrils, winding around Hydra's power. I could take all of this from her. I could be the great sea witch that everyone feared. Even greater than the last surviving Dark One—The Sea Serpent.

I could be that beautiful creature from my dreams.

Hydra stared at me, her eyes wide. "This is all *mine,*" she hissed, still struggling against my power. Her black and white snakes were spewing venom and their eyes were mesmerizing emerald green. They were undulating so fluidly, it almost broke my focus.

I moved toward her slowly, relishing the feeling of total control, enjoying the way she cowered. "You killed my parents," I said, my voice low and dangerous. "You killed my grandfather. You destroyed my family…and now, you're going to pay."

Raising my arms, I squeezed my hands into fists

and pulled down in a tearing motion. Hydra let out a primal scream of pain, and a split-second later, a blast of her power nearly knocked me over. I lost my grip, and in that moment, Hydra grabbed her rod. It glowed a fierce bright green, and she raised it high, ready to deliver the same blow to me as she had to Grandfather.

"Violet!"

At the sound of Tristan's voice, I glanced over just in time to see him toss Grandfather's sword to me. I caught it with a triumphant cry and spun around, defending myself from Hydra's blow. She snarled, her eyes wide and wild, and we began to duel.

I had never dueled before, but I had watched Grandfather's men during their training sessions. I darted from side to side, dodging blow after blow, waiting for the right moment to deliver one of my own. But Hydra was stronger than me, and her rod was infused with her power...

An idea came to me, and I didn't give myself a chance to second-guess it. Squeezing the hilt, I focused all my efforts on sending my powers into the sword. Hydra faltered as it began to glow a dull purple. I concentrated harder, and soon the sword was encased in a blindingly bright light the exact color of the amethyst. It reflected back on me, turning my arms purple, and my legs, and soon I felt the glow on my face as well.

I drew back, then swiped at Hydra with all of my strength.

The blow of power sent her flying high, high up into the ship's mast, where she was tangled up in the wind-torn sails. She dropped her rod, and it fell to the floor of the ship. I felt Hydra's powers extinguish...

...and then, with the groan of a dying giant, the ship fell back to the ocean.

Screams and shouts filled the air as the ship lurched forward, a great wave crashing over the side and flooding the deck. I stumbled forward, still clutching Grandfather's sword, trying to regain my balance.

"Tristan! *Tristan!*" I shouted, panicking. All around me, men were yelling, tripping, a few even falling over the railing and toppling into the ocean. I saw a few grab Grandfather's body and drag him to the cabin—and there was Sirena, her arms tight around Tristan. My shoulders slumped with relief as she made her way into the cabin with him.

Turning away, I ran to the bow of the ship and gazed out at the horrifying sight in front of me. The whirlpool had lost its electric green glow, but even without Hydra's powers, it had too much momentum to simply stop now. It was a great, black hole, a vortex in the middle of the water—and we were already circling it like a drowning ant circling the drain in a bathtub.

My stomach flipped over as I tried to think. Hydra's powers had started this whirlpool...maybe my powers could stop it. Closing my eyes, I focused as hard as I could on the whirlpool, imagining the bright purple light of my powers that had enveloped Grandfather's sword extending into the whirlpool. I could feel the incredible force of the water in my bones, and every muscle in my body tensed as I used my powers to make it slow...

...slow...

...slow...

...*stop*.

I collapsed to my knees, gasping for breath. Overhead, the gray clouds drifted away, revealing a bright blue sky. The ship rocked back and forth on the still-choppy sea, but the whirlpool was gone.

After a few moments, I managed to get to my feet and turn around. A few men lying on the deck moaned and began to sit up, looking around in confusion. The ship's mast had snapped in two, the top half dangling, the sail ripped and flapping in the breeze. And Hydra was gone.

I stared around warily, but there was no sign of her. I couldn't shake the feeling that she was still present. That she was watching me. I could *feel* her fury that I'd defeated her.

The door to the main cabin creaked open, and Sirena poked her head out.

"It's over?" she whispered, and it came out like a question.

I didn't answer. *Was* it over?

The guards eyed me warily. They didn't look nearly as relieved as I felt, and I knew why. The windmill incident had been enough to convince people I was a witch. This had been a whole new level of power. Yes, I had defeated Hydra when even Grandfather couldn't—but that didn't make me a hero in the guards' eyes. It made them suspicious.

Tristan appeared next to Sirena, bracing himself on the door jamb. His eyes met mine, and his face lit up with a grin.

"Violet, you did it! You saved us all!"

For a wonderful, fleeing moment, I forgot all about the guards, allowed myself to believe him. I had saved everyone. I *was* a hero.

Then the ship lurched, rocking back and forth as if a great creature beneath the surface had bumped up against it. Before I could react, Hydra's voice rumbled around us like thunder.

"*Violet Kronborg, your family owes me a debt you have barely begun to repay.*"

Shouts of terror filled the air as an enormous green hand, larger than a whale, rose up out of the water. I threw myself to the deck as those awful, massive fingers sailed over my head—and plucked Tristan up like he was nothing more than a grape.

"*No!*" I screamed, and then I was running and wielding Grandfather's sword, Sirena right on my heels, but I was too late, and the last thing I saw were Tristan's wide, terrified eyes before the hand dragged him into the sea.

I flew toward the railing, fully intending on jumping in after him, but then a great cracking noise overhead caused me to falter. I looked up just as the top half of the broken mast fell…straight toward me.

There was an explosion of stars behind my eyes, and then I was lost in a black abyss of nothingness.

19

AWOKE

"Tris…"

My tongue felt like a fat slug in my mouth. I was flat on my back, surrounded by darkness. Was I back in Hydra's cave? Why did I feel so groggy? Maybe this was what it felt like to be cursed. Maybe Grandfather had cursed me. Maybe Poseidon had dragged me down here to the coldest, darkest part of the ocean. I heard myself let out a moan.

"Tristan…"

Tristan. I was worried about him. Was he here in the cave with me? I couldn't think straight, couldn't remember anything.

I rolled my head to the side, groaning again. My eyelids scratched like sandpaper. With great effort, I managed to open my eyes just a tiny bit—then immediately squeezed them closed against the bright light.

So, I wasn't in the cave, then. And now that I thought about it, that felt like a pillow beneath my head. I was in bed. *My* bed. Had everything just been a terrible nightmare? Memories swam in my mind all out of order: Hydra in my bedroom, conjuring the ocean; a great green hand rising from the waves; the open jaws of a shark closing around me; the angry hiss of an otter; a gleaming purple gem in my palm; Grandfather falling to the deck; my parents' sunken ship; Tristan throwing me a sword; Tristan cheering me on; Tristan, Tristan...

"Tristan!"

I sat bolt upright, then instantly regretted it. My bedroom spun wildly around me, and I heard footsteps outside my door, and then a wonderful, familiar voice cried:

"Violet!"

"Cora," I managed to choke out as she rushed to my side. Cora's face was stark white as she placed a hand on my back.

"You need to rest, Miss Violet," she whispered. "You took quite a blow to the head."

As if in response to her words, the back of my head

began to throb painfully. I swallowed, my throat dry and scratchy, and leaned into Cora.

"What happened?"

Cora paused a moment before responding. "You don't remember? You were on the ship, and…Mom said the mast broke. It fell and…oh, it hit you in the head, Miss Violet, and we all thought…we were all so afraid that you were..."

I inhaled sharply, remembering the great, jagged piece of wood falling from the sky. I had been running, running across the deck, intending to jump over the side because…because…

"Oh, no," I said, my voice cracking. Hot tears filled my eyes. "Tristan is…he's really…gone?"

Cora let out a soft sob, and that was all I needed to hear.

Tristan was lost to the ocean. After all I went through, I had failed to save him.

She pulled me close, and we wept together. *I'm so sorry, Tristan,* I thought over and over again. *I'm so sorry.*

When my sobs turned dry and hoarse and I began to hiccup, I finally pulled away from Cora. Her eyes were bloodshot, but she gave me a watery smile.

"I'm so grateful you're safe, Miss Violet," she said, tucking the silver lock of hair behind my ears. "I don't know what I would've done if we'd lost you both."

I tried to return her smile, but I lowered my gaze. I was afraid if Cora could see into my eyes, she'd know the truth: that I would rather be in the ocean with Tristan.

"Is your mother okay?" I whispered.

Cora sighed. "She's…well, she's coping. She's the toughest person I know."

My throat ached as I remembered the way Sirena had watched Grandfather duel Hydra, her hands clasped to her heart. "Did you…did you know?" I asked quietly. "That your mother and my grandfather were in love?"

Something odd flickered in Cora's expression, and for a moment I wondered if I'd made a mistake in mentioning it.

"You mean *are* in love," she corrected me.

I stared at her, my confusion lasting longer than perhaps it should have. Surely, she didn't mean…

"Is…is he…" I swallowed hard. "Is my grandfather *alive*?"

Cora nodded slowly. "Yes. He's alive. But…"

I buried my face in my hands again, fresh tears streaming down my cheeks. Only now I was crying from happiness. The image of Hydra slashing Grandfather's chest, of his eyes widening in shock as he fell, played over and over again in my mind. I had been so sure he was dead.

"Here, Miss Violet," Cora said, picking up a small

vial of something chalky white on my bedside table. "The medic said you were to drink this as soon as you woke up. It'll help with the pain."

Dutifully, I took the vial and drained it, gagging slightly at the sour taste. Setting the vial down, I took a deep breath. "I want to see Grandfather."

Cora leaned forward. "Listen. You need to know that—"

"I have to see him." I was already trying to stand, my legs quaking with the effort. "Now."

"No, you need to rest, miss!" Cora sounded close to tears again as she placed her hands on my shoulders. I shrugged her off, pulling my robe on.

"I can rest later. I need to see Grandfather. I have to tell him—"

"You can't tell him anything," Cora interrupted. Twin spots of red had bloomed on her already rosy cheeks.

I stared at her blankly. "What do you mean?"

"I mean…" Cora looked around my room helplessly, smoothing down her apron. "I mean you can talk to him all you like, but he can't hear you. He's unconscious, miss. Has been since you all arrived back at the castle."

My heart sank. I stood there, my head pounding terribly. The room began to sway, and Cora reached out and caught me as I tilted sideways.

"There we go, now," she whispered, helping me

back into bed. "You just rest up, okay? I'll go fix you a nice cup of tea."

I nodded feebly as she bustled out of the room. Alone once again, I turned my attention to the window. I could see the half-built wall between the castle and the sea, a sliver of the glittering waters still visible. I wondered if Grandfather's men would continue working on it while he recovered.

If he recovered.

A scuttling noise caught my attention, and I looked over at my door just as Flotsam and Jetsam scurried in. They leaped onto the bed and clamored for my attention, Flotsam lavishing my arms and face with kisses while Jetsam snuggled up right against my belly. For the first time since I'd woken up, I found myself smiling, and I held my pups tightly.

My gaze wandered back to that sliver of sea. I couldn't bear the thought of Tristan as Hydra's prisoner. But I couldn't bear the thought of him being dead, either. Which would be worse for him? For me?

And the pearl…I groaned out loud as I remembered the shiny white orb drifting away from my reach, lost to the ocean. Even once I regained my strength, I wouldn't be able to search for Tristan. Not unless I somehow figured out how to use my powers to breathe underwater.

The more I thought about Tristan, the more I felt as though my skeleton was trying to claw its way out of my skin. I couldn't take this anymore, lying here in bed and doing nothing. Carefully, I dislodged myself from Flotsam and Jetsam and slid out of bed, leaving them curled up together next to my pillow. The room still swayed, but I lifted my chin and tightened the belt on my robe. Dizziness or no, I had to see Grandfather.

Halfway down the hall, I heard Cora returning with a tea tray. I hid behind a suit of armor until she passed, then made my way to the king's bedchambers. Soft voices came from within, and I hesitated just outside the doors.

"The council will be meeting later to decide on a course of action." Emil's sniveling voice made me grit my teeth. "The people of Elsinore do not yet know of the king's fate, but this cannot be kept secret forever."

"I'll remind you that we do not know the king's fate, either," Sirena replied, her tone cool. "Unless you have soothsayer powers the court is unaware of. He may yet recover, Emil."

Emil was silent for a moment. "And I'll remind you that the castle chef does not have authority or influence over such matters, or indeed over anything outside of the kitchen. No matter what her... *relationship* to the king might be."

Sirena let out a humorless laugh. "Is that the way it's going to be, you little runt?" she taunted, and

I almost laughed out loud. "As if you didn't waste years pining over Lydian. The king hasn't guessed how you felt about her, but I know."

My mouth fell open in shock. Emil had been in love with my mother? I remembered how angry he'd been at Grandfather in the west wing right after Tristan had disappeared. *Because of your foolish deal, Lydian was...* His voice had trembled with emotion when he'd uttered her name. I wrinkled my nose in disgust.

"Go on now, run to your meeting and pretend you're king, like we all know you want to be. We'll see what happens when this land's true leader wakes up and hears what you've been up to."

A deadly silence followed this. I was suddenly glad I couldn't see Emil's expression. When he replied, his voice was no more than a hiss.

"Yes. We'll see what happens."

This was followed by footsteps growing closer, and I ducked back just as the door flew open. I peered around it, watching Emil stalk down the hall.

I hovered there for a moment, one foot inside Grandfather's chambers. But as I watched Emil's retreating back, everything I'd overheard in the library's secret passage came flooding back to me.

We must do what is best for Elsinore.

The king has brought this misery on himself. Ever since the war against the Dark Ones, the pact with

Poseidon, the king has been keeping a grave secret from all of us. One that puts Elsinore at risk more and more every day.

The girl is a ticking time bomb. Already, everyone in Elsinore suspects the truth about her. All this past year, I thought the king simply couldn't admit it, was too blinded by love for his granddaughter. But the real truth is far, far worse.

I pictured the unfinished wall outside and remembered interrupting the council meeting and confronting Grandfather.

Out of sight, out of mind. You will not look at the ocean. You will not think of the ocean. You will not dream of the ocean. You will focus on your studies and on becoming the queen Elsinore expects you to be—the queen they will one day need *you to be.*

Finally, I thought of Grandfather's desperate, pleading expression on the ship when he'd told me the truth about the curse. That only a marriage between land and sea would seal it and cement Hydra's doom. My marriage to Poseidon's son, Triton.

My mother had tried to convince him to leave me out of it, and Grandfather had ignored him. She had gone to Poseidon instead, and Hydra had drowned her and my father. They had died for me. My parents had died so that I could be free to make my own choices.

And Emil *knew* all of this. He had been in love

231

with my mother, and he knew she had sacrificed her life for mine. No wonder he hated me so much. No wonder he hated Grandfather. No wonder...

Another bout of dizziness hit me, and I grabbed the wall for support. *No wonder he wanted to commit treason.*

The king was unconscious and might not recover. This was the chance Emil had been waiting for.

Leaving Grandfather's chambers behind, I shook off the lingering dizziness and sprinted to the council chamber as fast as my legs would carry me.

20

TREASON

No need for a covert meeting with a few treasonous members this time. Emil had called an emergency session. I lurked behind a column, watching as the council members trooped inside the chambers, grim-faced and pale. Before the doors closed, I slipped in after them, ducking behind a suit of armor.

Last time, I had barged in here to confront Grandfather, and it did not go well. I remembered the way Hydra had hidden in the shadows of the cave when I'd found Tristan and showed him the gems. *Keep still and silent, and learn what your enemy is up to before you confront them,* I told myself firmly. Hydra might have been evil, but she was also extremely clever. I figured I might as well use one or two of the tricks she had taught me.

Emil took his seat at the head of the long table. *Grandfather's* seat. I gritted my teeth as I stared at his somber expression. He wasn't fooling me one bit. I could see the way his lips quirked up in a faint, but definitely smug, smile.

To his right, the reedy-looking man stood up.

"This meeting of the king's council is now in session," he announced. "Due to the king's condition, senior advisor Emil Jensen will be presiding."

"Thank you, Rodden," Emil said gravely. "Fellow council members, I will not mince words. Our king lies gravely injured, and our kingdom is under attack."

A murmur rippled down the table as the men shifted uncomfortably in their chairs.

"You have all no doubt heard rumors of what transpired out at sea yesterday." Emil lifted his chin and looked around. "The king's guards were themselves witnesses, and I have heard testimony from each and every one of them. So, I want to take this opportunity to dispel the rumors and give you the full truth of what happened."

A shiver ran up my spine as I recalled the way the guards had looked at me. I had saved their lives, I reminded myself. But uncertainty unspooled in my gut as I listened to Emil.

"One of the Dark Ones survived, and she has returned."

Shouts and cries of disbelief rang out. I chewed my lip as Emil raised his hands for silence.

"Hydra the sea witch was the last of her family," he said. "During the great war, our beloved king knew that Elsinore was fighting a losing battle against the Dark Ones. He turned to Poseidon, King of the sea, and they forged a pact in secret."

The council members were rapt with attention. So was I, even though I already knew this part of the story.

"The pact involved a curse that would trap the last Dark One in the deepest trench in the ocean," Emil went on. "But such a powerful curse required something equally powerful to hold it in place. The unification of land and sea through the bond of marriage. Poseidon's young son and the king's granddaughter were to forge that bond. The pact was signed, the deal was done."

Emil paused, and a complicated expression flickered across his face.

"Two years ago, our princess and her husband set sail," he said, his lip curling up ever so slightly on the word *husband.* "They wanted to meet the young prince to whom their daughter was betrothed."

That's not why they went, I thought angrily,

squeezing my hands into fists. *They wanted to convince Poseidon to keep me out of the curse.*

"Unfortunately, in doing so, they also gave Poseidon the opportunity he had been waiting for," Emil continued. "The king of the sea never wanted to share power, after all. The power of the Dark Ones was the greater foe—but make no mistake, Poseidon always thought of Elsinore as a foe as well."

I shook my head vigorously, remembering my mother's words in her letter. *Our kingdoms have always been the greatest of allies.*

"He did not want to see his only son married to a human girl," Emil said. "And so, he drowned our princess in an open act of war."

More cries of shock rang out, including my own. It took all of my willpower not to leap out from my hiding place and call Emil out on his lies. Hydra had drowned my parents, not Poseidon. Why was he saying this?

Patience. Let your enemy spill his secrets before you make your move.

Crouching down lower, I continued to listen.

"We all suffered a great loss that day," Emil said, his voice cracking with emotion. "But none more so than the king. In all truth, he never recovered from Princess Lydian's death. For months, I hoped that his condition would improve. But he has only become more…unhinged."

"Unhinged?" a council member with white-blond hair said with a frown. "He grieved, yes, but his sanity is intact, surely."

Emil sighed heavily. "Alas, no. And this is where I'm afraid I must take the blame."

I wrinkled my nose. Surely the council members could see straight through this phony act? But they all stared at Emil intently as he continued.

"I first began to notice the signs nearly a year ago," Emil said. "After the...incident on the princess's birthday."

My stomach turned over. The storm. The windmill. *Witch.*

"Those who witnessed the event could not believe their eyes," Emil went on. "The princess, the future queen, exposing unholy powers, ripping a windmill out of the ground and nearly killing them."

My mouth dropped. I hadn't *summoned* the windmill, I had *banished* it! I had saved my life and everyone else's!

"But of course, to say such things constitutes as treason," Emil said. "The people were afraid to speak up. They hoped, as did I, that the king would take appropriate action."

He let out another world-weary sigh.

"Alas, the king decided to protect her instead. To ignore the fact that the girl was a danger. To put his own people, *our* people, at risk instead of confronting the *truth*!"

His voice rose passionately, the word *truth* echoing off the marble walls. Emil waited until the word had faded and the hall was silent. He looked around the table, holding each council members' gaze briefly.

"But the truth can only be concealed for so long," Emil went on quietly. "As I said, I have long suspected it, and I should have acted. But the guards present on the ship yesterday confirmed my deepest fears. Hydra is a great enemy of Elsinore, it is true. So is Poseidon. But our greatest enemy is within these walls."

I felt numb as I waited for his next words, even though I knew exactly what they would be.

"Ursula Violet Kronborg."

21

TRINITY STONE

The dizziness returned with a vengeance, threatening to overtake me. I struggled to take deep, long breaths while staying as still as possible. Several council members were arguing loudly with Emil, whose gaze moved around the table....and, for the briefest of moments, seemed to lock with my own.

I moved further back into the shadows, heart pounding wildly as his eyes moved on. He hadn't actually *seen* me, I reassured myself. Only the suit of armor.

Meanwhile, the council was in an uproar.

"Surely not!"

"She will be our queen one day!"

"She saved the king's life!"

Emil raised his hands again. "Gentlemen, believe me. I know this is difficult to hear. But the guards witnessed the event themselves. The princess has unnatural powers. At such a young age, she was able to defeat Hydra when even King Kronborg could not. However…"

He paused, his expression one of mock regret, and my mouth turned sour.

"Hydra was only there because Violet released her from her curse. The guards heard her confess it all to King Kronborg. The girl admitted to turning the sea witch loose on her own grandfather. On her *king*. Because she knew that if he died, she would take the throne."

This time, it was all I can do not to cry out in shock. That sniveling rat was implying that *I wanted Grandfather dead!* That I had retrieved the gems for Hydra not to save Tristan, but to kill the king! Fury bubbled hot inside me, and I wanted nothing more in that moment than to lash out with my powers and send Emil flying out of a window.

Cold sweat broke out on my brow, and I struggled to maintain my composure. At least now I understood why the guards had looked so afraid. They had witnessed my confrontation with Grandfather, when he'd learned I broke Hydra's curse by giving her the gems. He had been terrified, and they thought it was because he feared for his own life.

Only Grandfather could tell them the real truth. But he was unconscious.

"But the princess was also hurt in the incident," the blond council member pointed out. "A serious injury, or so we were told."

Emil let out a humorless chuckle. "Indeed. Because as the sea witch retreated into the ocean and the king lay dying, do you know what the princess did?" He placed his hands on the table and glowered at the council. "She abandoned her grandfather and attempted to *follow the witch.*"

The blond council member looked startled. "Surely she was attempting to save her cousin?"

Emil pounded the table with his fist so loudly, even I jumped. "We must stop making excuses for this girl's treacherous actions! She unleashed the last surviving Dark One on Elsinore, on the king. She wants *power*, don't you see? She would have followed Hydra into the depths to regroup and launch a fresh attack, had the mast not knocked her out. And her injury was not life-threatening."

He lowered his voice, dark eyes flashing.

"The girl must no longer be allowed to run amok, her powers unchecked. And though it pains me to say this, King Kronborg is not fit to decide what to do about her. He is too soft-hearted. Had he taken

241

appropriate action last year, all of this—Tristan's death, Hydra's attack—would have never come to pass. We must stiffen our resolve and do what is best for Elsinore."

"And what is that?" another council member asked.

Emil gestured to Rodden, who got to his feet and cleared his throat.

"As acting senior counsel, I hereby call for a vote on the Emergency Succession Act to name Emil Jensen as King and ruler of Elsinore."

The shouts and cries all faded, and my vision blurred around the edges. I felt as if I was falling into some endless abyss. *We were right, Tristan,* I thought miserably. *Emil is plotting a coup. And he's about to succeed.*

I remembered huddling under my blankets the night Tristan and I had spied on Emil. I remembered my chamber doors opening as I fought to stay still, to control my breathing. Now I pictured Emil standing there, smiling that smug smile. He couldn't prove that I had been the one spying on him, but it didn't matter. He had already put his plan to take the throne in place.

And everything I had done since then—my outburst at the party, breaking into the west wing to find the pearl, fetching the gems and freeing Hydra—had ensured his plan would succeed beyond his wildest dreams.

"Gentlemen, please," Emil said gravely, and silence fell once more. "This gives me no pleasure at all, believe me. But I implore you to look at the facts. King Kronborg suffered a deadly blow from the last surviving Dark One, and the royal medic tells me he very well may not recover. This sea witch has also claimed the life of Tristan Kronborg and is no doubt plotting her next move. Elsewhere in the ocean, Poseidon is watching, waiting for Elsinore to fall."

I peered out from behind the suit of armor, as the council members nodded, their expressions all of grim resolve.

"Our enemies gain strength while our king is barely breathing," Emil said, his voice rising. "In this moment, who do you think should lead the great people of Elsinore? The king's senior and most trusted advisor, or the wicked girl who put these wheels in motion to begin with? The girl who is even as I speak is *lurking in these very chambers*?"

I comprehended the meaning of his last words a split-second too late. Emil pointed at the suit of armor—at *me*—and every single council member sprang to their feet and stared at me in horror.

I was paralyzed with fear. Dimly, I tried to tell myself to use my powers, to run, to do *anything*. But it was as if I was a tree with roots planted deep into the castle floor.

243

No, wait. This was more than just fear. The dizziness had been growing steadily worse ever since I left my bedchambers. Something was wrong with me.

"Seize her." Emil beckoned the guard in the corner with an almost careless gesture.

A hush fell as the guard moved toward me, the *clomp-clomp-clomp* of his boots in time with the thumping of my heart. *Fight him,* I told myself frantically. *Send a blast of power at him. You defeated Hydra, the last of the Dark Ones! You can handle a mere guard!*

But it was no use. The room spun around and around, and I couldn't even summon the strength to get to my feet. I sat there like a lump on a log as the guard approached, struggling just to stay conscious. When the guard grabbed my arm, I gave up and succumbed to the darkness.

I awoke hours later in my bed, covered in sweat. Outside, the sun had set, stars beginning to shine in the deep purple sky.

"Violet! You're awake, thank goodness."

Startled, I saw Sirena getting up from the armchair in the corner and rushing over to me. I let out a weak sob of relief as she me into a hug. I clung to her, breathing in the warm scent of freshly baked bread and flowers. Then I pulled away, gripping her arms urgently.

"Sirena, Emil is a traitor. He's—"

"I know, dear. I know." Sirena sighed, and I saw how pale her face was. "The council unanimously voted to enact the Emergency Succession Act."

I stared at her in horror. "You mean…Emil is *King*?"

"Not exactly," Sirena said quickly. "More like *acting* king while the true king is…recovering. Your grandfather is still the rightful king of Elsinore—or he will be, when he wakes up."

"When will that be?" I asked desperately. "What did the medics say?"

Sirena's voice broke when she responded. "That weapon Hydra used was no ordinary sword. We believe it must have been cursed. The medics are at a loss of what to do to help him. They've tried everything, Violet. He's still breathing, but…"

She trailed off, so I finished her thought. "But they don't think he'll wake up."

Sirena sighed. "We mustn't give up hope, Violet. Especially now, with Emil…" Her face darkened. "I never trusted him, never. I tried to warn Eric so many times, but Emil had been his advisor for so long, well before we…" She stopped, casting me a sideways glance.

I couldn't help but smile. "Before you fell in love?"

Sirena let out a dry laugh. "Is it that obvious?"

"You weren't exactly subtle about it," I teased, and she swatted me on the arm. "Sirena, I—I need to see him."

"No." Sirena's voice was firm and her smile vanished. "Violet, listen to me. The council debated on what to do with you. A few of them wanted to throw you in the dungeons. But Emil convinced them that it would be best if you were confined to your chambers for the time being."

I frowned. "I'm surprised Emil didn't jump at the chance to lock me up in the dungeons."

Sirena shook her head. "He's crafty, that one. He doesn't want to appear too eager to replace the king. He has to make it look as though he's only doing this because Eric is ill and you are a threat to the kingdom."

A threat to the kingdom. Bitterness rose in my throat. Emil Jensen had all but accused me of staging a coup, when he had been the one plotting to overthrow the king the entire time. The injustice stung.

"If you're caught sneaking around again—if you…" Sirena paused, her gaze dropping to her hands. I knew what she was thinking, and I felt a flush of guilt. *If you use your powers to hurt anyone again.* "Well, sweetheart, we don't want to give Emil a reason to do something even worse. Okay?"

I wanted to argue. But instead, I nodded. "Okay. I

understand. And Sirena?" My cheeks warmed when she looked up at me. "I'm so sorry for what I did to you on the ship," I whispered, tears springing to my eyes. "I was angry, but...but that's no excuse."

Sirena leaned forward and wrapped her arms around me. I buried my face in her shoulder as she whispered, "I know, my love. It's all right."

She pulled away, wiping a tear from her eye, and stood. "Now, I need to get back to the kitchens," she said. "I'm sure Emil would love a reason to fire me, and I don't plan to give him one by slacking off up here with you."

She winked before turning to leave, and I tried to smile. But her words had sent a fresh ripple of fear through me. I remembered the conversation I'd overheard between her and Emil. Their dislike for one another was obvious. She was right—Emil would be happy to get rid of her. And if Sirena left, that meant Cora would be gone, too. And I would have no allies left in this castle.

I would be all alone.

"Oh, hon," Sirena called from the door. "The medic left another dose of pain medicine there for you. Don't forget to take it."

"Okay," I said dully, and she closed the door. I made a face at the vial of chalky-white stuff. Painkiller or not, I didn't relish the thought of drinking it again.

I also didn't relish the thought of wasting away

in my chambers while Emil sat on Grandfather's throne.

Throwing off the covers, I hurried to my closet and stripped off my nightgown. I dug through my dresses until I found my riding outfit—the most comfortable outfit I owned.

Once I was dressed, I crept to my door and pushed it open just a crack. As I suspected, a guard stood watch at the end of the hall, blocking my way to Grandfather's chambers.

I turned to face my room, my eyes scanning over my dresser and bed before landing on the vial on my night table. *Perfect.* Grabbing the vial, I returned to the door and pushed it open just far enough to fit my arm through. I took aim in the opposite direction of the guard and hurled the vial as hard as I could, slipping back in my room and closing the door a split-second before I heard it smash against the stone.

"Who's there?" called the guard. I peered through my cracked-open door as he rushed past, then slipped and sprinted in the opposite direction.

There were no guards outside Grandfather's chambers, which I thought was odd...until I pushed the door open and saw Emil speaking to the royal medic at Grandfather's bedside.

I froze, listening to their hushed voices.

"...every four hours should do it," the medic was saying. "Every six hours for the girl."

"Excellent." Emil sounded pleased. "A little something for your troubles."

I watched as he handed the medic a small sack. The medic tucked it in his pocket, and I heard the rattle of coins.

"Many thanks, your highness." The medic winked, and Emil chuckled.

I ducked behind the door as they left Grandfather's side, flattening myself against the wall as the door swung open, concealing me. As they walked down the hall, I slipped inside right before the door clicked closed.

My stomach dropped when I saw Grandfather. He looked so small and frail in the great big bed. His face was deathly pale, as did the bony hands resting on top of the thick layers of blankets. There were dark shadows beneath his eyes, and his cheeks were so sunken in he almost looked like a skeleton. His snow-white hair, thick and wavy the last time I'd seen him on the ship, now hung in limp, lanky locks that grazed his shoulders.

How did this happen? I thought desperately as I hurried to his side. Grandfather had been unconscious last time I saw him, but now he looked as though he was wasting away. Had Hydra's sword really been cursed?

My gaze drifted to the vial of chalk-white liquid on his bedside, and suddenly, I knew.

249

Emil had bribed the medic. That vial wasn't filled with a painkiller. Whatever was in it had caused my dizziness, had made me pass out in the council chambers. No wonder Emil hadn't looked worried about me overpowering the guard. He'd had me *drugged.*

And he was drugging Grandfather, too. All so he could stay in power.

For a moment, my fury threatened to overwhelm me. Then I reached out and lay my hand on top of Grandfather's.

His eyelashes twitched.

I gasped, leaning closer. "Grandfather? Can you hear me?"

I watched, hardly daring to breathe, as Grandfather's lids fluttered open. His blue eyes were out of focus for a few seconds before his gaze locked onto mine.

"Tr…"

"Grandfather," I whispered, squeezing his hands with mine. Hope buoyed me for the first time all day. "It's okay."

"Tri…"

Tristan. He was trying to say Tristan's name. I fought back yet another wave of tears. I couldn't bear the thought of telling Grandfather what had happened to Tristan, not while he was in such a fragile state. "It's okay," I said again, even though nothing was okay. "You need to rest. Don't strain yourself."

But Grandfather was attempting to sit up now. His eyes never left mine as his mouth tried desperately to form words. I tried to help him rest back against the pillow, but he struggled against me. Finally, he drew a deep, rattling breath, and uttered one word.

"*Trinity.*"

Then his eyes fluttered closed, and he collapsed back against the pillow, utterly motionless.

For a moment, I feared the worst had happened. Then Grandfather let out a soft sigh, his chest rising and falling gently.

"What does that mean?" I whispered. But even as I said it, realization was starting to dawn.

Trinity.

The day before my birthday—a full lifetime ago, or at least it felt that way—I had burst into the library to tell Tristan about the wall. And he'd slid the book he was reading out of sight before he'd realized it was me. A black book with a gold triangle on the front.

Pretty sure I'd get in plenty of trouble reading a book of spells.

Cora had interrupted us before Tristan could tell me more about the book. And I'd been so consumed with the wall that I'd forgotten all about it later. But now I was starting to put the pieces together. Tristan had known since my tenth birthday that I had powers, ever since he saw what I did to the windmill. He hadn't told me because he didn't want to upset me, but he had been researching *magic.*

And Tristan hadn't found that book of spells in the library—he'd told me so himself. He'd been snooping around the forbidden west wing right before my birthday. The wing filled with all sorts of things Grandfather didn't want us to see…like all of my parents' books, which he had locked up in the Solar.

A wild and crazy thought seized me. Had Tristan found that strange book of spells in the Solar?

Had that book belonged to my *parents*?

Shouts and footsteps out in the hall caught my attention. I sprang to my feet, giving Grandfather a kiss on the forehead.

"Don't give up hope, Grandfather," I whispered fiercely. "I'm going to take our kingdom back."

I raced to the doors and peered outside. Sure enough, several guards were sprinting down the hall toward my chambers. My absence had been discovered.

I didn't have much time.

I ran flat-out for Tristan's chambers. The sight of his organized shelves, his neatly made bed, his clothes hanging in the open closet, felt like a knife piercing my heart. I stopped and looked around, trying to think logically. Tristan would have hidden the book. Someplace Cora wouldn't come across when she was cleaning.

Hurrying over to his bed, I stuck my hand beneath the mattress. My fingers closed around a book, and I let out a triumphant cry as I pulled it out.

The gold triangle shimmered on the black cover. *Trinity,* I thought, opening the book and flipping through the pages.

Spells. Page after page of spells. And in the margins were notes written in familiar looping script.

"Mother," I whispered in awe, running my fingers over her words. She had studied this book. She had studied *magic.*

I could feel my power swelling inside me as I sank to Tristan's bed, holding the book reverently. Maybe it doesn't matter that I lost the pearl. Maybe with this book, I didn't need it.

I just needed to learn how to properly use my powers. I could fight Hydra and win. I could save Tristan. I could save Grandfather. I could save all of Elsinore.

And I would.

As I closed the book, an ocean-blue glint caught my eye. Startled, I opened the book to the very back and gasped.

Embedded in the back of the book, twinkling up at me, was a *sapphire.*

My mind whirled. What did this mean? Was it

another one of the Dark Ones' gems? Why would my mother have it? And what did Grandfather want me to do with it?

The floor shook as more guards ran up to the third floor. I was out of time.

Closing my eyes, I sent out a silent call. *Come quick, as fast as you can. I need you.*

Then, clutching my mother's book tightly, I marched to the doors and threw them open.

"I'm right here!" I called as I walked into the hall. Moments later, the guards had surrounded me. Emil came forward, gazing at me with an expression of mock concern.

"Now, what are you doing out here?" he chided. "I went out on a limb for you, Violet Kronborg. I told everyone that surely, after all the trouble you had caused, you would remain in your chambers. You need to recover. You need rest."

I smiled. "Actually, I'm feeling much better. Especially after I got rid of that so-called painkiller you drugged me with."

The blood drained from Emil's face. I could practically see him realize what this meant. If I wasn't drugged, I might just be able to use my powers after all.

"Lies," he hissed. "Perhaps a night in the dungeons will teach you a thing or two."

I ignored him and looked around at the guards.

"Emil bribed the royal medic to drug the king," I said in a loud, clear voice. "Test his painkillers if you don't believe me."

Most of the guards glared at me. But I saw a few shift nervously, casting glances at Emil. Good. He didn't have their full loyalty just yet. There was still hope.

"Enough of this nonsense," Emil snapped. "Take her to—"

But his words were lost under the rumble of horse hooves. There were shouts and cries of shock as the guards blocking the staircase leaped out of the way.

I beamed as Sprites galloped down the hall, bright red mane streaming behind her. Emil's face went from white to purple as I leaped up onto the magnificent horse's back.

"Enjoy the throne while you have it, you traitor," I said, relishing the fear that flashed in his eyes. "You won't have it for long."

And Sprites took off, barreling through the guards, carrying me down the stairs and out the castle into the night, toward the ocean.

Toward my freedom.

About the Author

Jess Gray was born and raised outside the town of Montrose, in the beautiful mountain state of Colorado. Jess owns several businesses and considers her family to be most important to her. If she isn't spending time with her friends and family, you can almost always find her enjoying her favorite little mountain town, Ridgway, Colorado. Trinity Stone, is Jess' first middle grade book in the *The Witch of the Sea* trilogy.

Made in the USA
Columbia, SC
27 August 2021